Star on the Rise

By

Anthony Potts

www.publishnation.co.uk

Eye on the Ball

The first book in the Liam Osborne series by Anthony Potts.
An Amazon best seller.

What the readers say:

'This book is a great read with nice insight from someone who clearly knows the game.'

'A good book especially for for boys at that age when they lose interest in reading. A good story line very believable and written by someone who knows the true story behind football.'

'If you love Football you will love this book. Its insight into the struggle to become a professional footballer is fascinating and so true to life.'

'Enjoyable read. any aspiring young footballers should read this for an insight into the harsh realities of competing for a contract.'

'It is evident from the start that he has lived and breathed what he has written about.'

'This book lifted the lid on the very gritty world of professional football. The characters are such that you root for, hate and sympathize with them all at once . As all good books can, this book transported me into Liam's shoes. I was there with him for the knocks, the laughs and the pain.'

'Fantastic insight into YTS football scheme in the early 90s all wrapped up in a real page-turner of a story.'

'Great story about a footballers rise from local football playing on the marshes to the first team at a second division club. Couldn't put it down.'

Find out more at anthonypottsauthor.com

For Sonya,

For all the support and encouragement.

Hope it was worth it!

1991-92

Chapter One

It was a scorching hot summer's day. The boy with the unruly mop of blonde hair came sprinting around the corner of the pitch and down the touchline, before coming to a stop in front of the entrance to the tunnel. Liam clasped his hands on to the top of his head and tried to slow his breathing. He felt good. He was as ready as he was ever going to be. The sweat dripped off his face and landed on the dirt track that encircled the pitch. He used the hem of his shirt to wipe the sweat off his face and out of his eyes. His bag and football were sitting in the dugout. He made for them, then grabbed his hoodie. It was feeling a little short in the arms, but it was the hood he needed. He looked around Clifton Park, home of Clifton Rangers. The pitch looked strange with no goalposts, more like a bowling green than a football pitch. He picked up his ball and stepped forward onto the edge of the grass, enjoying the feel of it below his feet.

"Off the grass Liam," came the exasperated shout.

"Sorry Ken," said Liam, stepping back and turning around, "It's so tempting. Can't I just kick the ball about a bit?"

Ken didn't even bother answering. Liam wasn't surprised. It wasn't the first time they had had this discussion. Other than a few workmen doing essential repairs around the stadium, the groundsman was the only Clifton Rangers employee Liam had seen during the whole of the off-season. This was an important time for Ken, a chance for the pitch to recover and for the new seed to grow. For six weeks, he was the most important person at the club.

Giving up, Liam picked up his bag, slung it over his shoulder and turned back to the pitch. It seemed like a lifetime since he had last played here in front of a crowd. It had been the game against Leyton, their local rivals. It was a full house. The atmosphere had been electric, it reminded the older fans of

Clifton's glory days. That had been the game that had confirmed Clifton Rangers' promotion to the First Division. The First Division. Liam had still been at Primary school the last time Clifton had been in the topflight. Despite only being a teenager, Liam had played practically every game the previous season. He was key to Clifton's chances of avoiding an immediate return to the Second Division.

He reached into his bag and pulled out his phone, he wasn't surprised to find that there were no missed calls. But he was still a little disappointed.

Tomorrow was the first day of preseason and Liam couldn't wait. It had felt like the longest summer of his life. He made his way back down the tunnel and out towards the reception. Today, like every other day of the summer, the place was deserted. The doors to the changing rooms were locked, as was the kit room. Johnny, the kitman, had only left Liam the keys to the tunnel, so he had to wait until he got home to change. Jesus, he even missed Johnny. Things must be bad. He made his way through reception into the car park checking to see if anyone was behind the reception, like a child checking a cupboard for an already-eaten chocolate bar.

As he turned into the high street, he paused. He pulled the hood over his head and tucked his chin into his chest. His walk quickened. Everywhere seemed to be clad in yellow and blue. The whole town had been in party mode since promotion had been achieved back in May. Every child seemed to be wearing the club shirt, and Rangers flags hung from every window. Liam glanced up, the Royal Oak's customers had spilled out onto the pavement, and were enjoying the sunshine. Liam thought about crossing the road, he even considered making a run for it. But it was too late.

"One Liam Osborne, there's only one Liam Osborne!" came the familiar chant.

At the start of the summer, he had almost enjoyed it, but now it cut right through him.

"'Ere he is, the little legend," said one of the group, a bearded man with a belly that stretched his Clifton Ranger's replica shirt to the seams.

"Come 'ave a drink with us," said another.

2

Liam politely declined, but his protests seemed to pass by unnoticed.

"Dave, get the boy a beer. He's one of our own this one."

"No, no honestly. I don't drink... thanks anyway," Liam said.

A pint was soon deposited in his hand, but by now it seemed like half the high street was there. Most of them were holding out various items dug out of bags for Liam to sign. Liam could feel his face reddening, he didn't think he would ever get used to it. It felt like he couldn't do anything without being mobbed these days. And he hated it. He was always happy to give his time to people, but he seemed to have the same conversations over and over again.

No, he couldn't wait to play against Mansford United and Tottenford.

Yes, he thought they could stay up.

No, he couldn't get them any tickets or shirts or tracksuits or pretty much any of the things they asked for.

Yes, Reg Varney really was as scary in real life as he seemed on the pitch.

No, they haven't signed any new players.

Most of the people he encountered he had never met before, yet they spoke to him with the familiarity of a family member, seemingly oblivious to his discomfort. The problem was everyone seemed to look at him differently, treated him differently, but he still felt like the same old Liam.

Eventually, he was able to tear himself away. His hand ached from all the items he had been made to sign.

"Thanks everyone, good to meet you all, but I've got to go," said Liam.

He could tell by the looks on their faces that there were a few people disappointed that he was leaving so quickly. It was like they felt they owned a bit of him. A couple of weeks previous, by mistake, he had missed one of the children who had been waiting for an autograph. The boy's dad had gone crazy. Shouting at Liam and telling him not to forget it was him and the other fans who paid Liam's wages. Afterwards, with the benefit of hindsight, Liam thought he should have asked for a raise as he was quite sure he was going to be the worst-paid player in the First Division next year.

Liam gave one last apologetic smile and continued up the high street.

"'Ere Dave, look at this. He never even touched his beer."

"Bloody typical, they think they're so special these bloody footballers," came the reply.

Chapter Two

The next morning, Liam still felt half asleep as he made his way through the huge iron gates and across the Clifton Park car park towards reception. In the past, he would have been looking out for Lisa, but now it was Jason he was looking for. He was hoping that Jason Blackmore or Greg Hales would still be catching the bus. If not, it was sure to be embarrassing being the only professional player on the youth team bus to training. Jason "Blackie" Blackmore had broken into the first team at about the same time as Liam and they had become great friends. There were times, when Liam had first joined the club, when it was only Jason's support that had kept him going. Greg Hales had been in the youth team with Jason and Liam. He had been given a one-year contract at the end of the previous season. When Liam had joined, Greg had been an example of all that was wrong with the club. He had been going through the motions waiting for good things to happen, more interested in what football could give him than what he could contribute. Now, in no small part due to the examples set by Liam and Jason, he had a work ethic to match his ability. His turnaround mirrored the turnaround in the fortunes of Clifton Rangers.

As Liam approached the main stand he glanced up, as he always did, at the huge letters spelling out Clifton Rangers that ran along the side of the West Stand. Even though this was his third season at the club, it still felt like a dream that he was sure he was going to wake from at any moment. His whole life he had been obsessed with football – more specifically Clifton Rangers. When he played in the playground, he was always a Clifton player whereas all his friends were Tottenford or Mansford United players. Every year his main Christmas present had been a replica Clifton Rangers shirt. Now he had his own replica shirt. It blew his mind to think this year there would be children asking for a Liam Osborne shirt.

Some of the new YTS boys were already sitting at the glass table in reception. They looked sick with fear. Liam made sure he gave an encouraging smile as he walked past. He could remember being in their position. It was moments of kindness that had helped get him through, and he would never forget that. He knew he was supposed to look down on the YTS boys. It was an unwritten rule in football that it was everyone's job to give them a hard time - the idea was to toughen them up. Make them pay their dues. It could be brutal. Liam had been told that Ryan Wilson, at Mansford United, had locked one of the YTS players in the skip that carried the kit. He had left him in there for hours. The YTS player had left the club the following week.

Feeling a little awkward, Liam decided to continue through to the kit room to see if Johnny needed any help. Johnny was unique at the club in the fact that he didn't care if you were a first year youth training scheme footballer or a senior professional. He didn't like anyone.

"Hi Johnny," said Liam nervously standing in the doorway.

"Hmmph," came the reply. Johnny didn't even turn around.

That's progress thought Liam as in the past Johnny would often have just ignored him.

"D'you want a hand?"

Without saying a word, Johnny slowly turned and closed the door.

"Can't believe I missed you," said Liam to the now closed door. Just quietly enough that Johnny wouldn't hear.

Liam made his way back out to the reception. There was now a large group of YTS boys standing around the tables. Shell suits were clearly the must-have clothing item for this year's youth team. You could spot the second years a mile off. They were loud, confident and animated. Meanwhile, the first years were all trying to blend into the background. He knew what that felt like. One or two of the second years nodded over to Liam, showing off in front of the first years. Liam nodded back but again aimed a smile in the direction of the nervous first-year players. It was now becoming clear that Greg and Jason must have been going straight to the training ground. Great, thought Liam, now he *would* be the only first team player on the bus. He decided to wait by the glass doors just out of view of the youth team. At 7.57, Johnny pulled the minibus up outside reception. He clambered off the bus and walked back past Liam and off through the door to the tunnel. He returned a minute later pushing the skip full of

6

the day's training kit. Liam followed him out the door and got onto the bus, taking the seat at the front adjacent to the driver – he knew no one ever took that seat. The boys all filed onto the bus. The second years all took the seats at the back while the first years took what was left. Liam smiled; he knew these were the seats that they would all be sitting in for the rest of the year. Footballers were notoriously territorial.

At exactly 8.00 Johnny closed the doors, nearly catching one unaware player in them as he did so. Then he was off.

"Hold up Johnny, here comes Tom," came a voice from the back.

Liam could see "Tom" come running through the gates towards the bus, but he already knew what was going to happen. The minibus seemed to speed up rather than slow down and the poor kid had to practically jump out the way. Liam felt sorry for him as he now had to try and make his own way to training - not a great first day. The older YTS boys showed no such sympathy.

"He's mugged you off Tommy!" came the shout followed by everyone banging on the back window and jeering. Tommy was already making his way off to the bus stop, giving the finger as he went. The rest of the journey was strangely comforting for Liam. He had come so far so quickly, there was something reassuring in seeing that some things had remained the same. They even had a go at the bell ringing game, where they tried to ring the bell as many times as they could without Johnny catching them.

"DING, DING, DING, DING!"

"Four's the record!" shouted Liam.

The scowl on Johnny's face as he turned to look at Liam reminded him why no-one ever sat next to the driver.

Chapter Three

Before too long, the minibus was swinging into the training ground and pulling up alongside the youth team huts. Liam let the youth team get off first as he knew they would be busy doing jobs around the training ground. The youth team players all had first team players' boots to clean, changing rooms to sweep out and footballs to be cleaned and pumped up ready for training. The first day of preseason was always the worst as, often at the end of a season, everything was just chucked away behind closed doors and forgotten about. Last year's YTS boys would have left a mess for this year's intake almost as a passing of the baton. Once the last of the players had passed, Liam nodded a pointless goodbye to Johnny and got off the bus. He made his way past the pond to the old Victorian house which served both as changing rooms and offices for the coaching staff. Liam had seen that Harry Welch, the first team manager, was here - his was the only car in the car park. Part of him wanted to go and see him and see how he was. He saw Harry as almost a father figure. Being a Rangers fan, Liam held Harry in the highest esteem. It was Harry who had first come to his mum's flat to tell him that he was going to have a trial with Clifton, and he knew that it was Harry's faith in him that had gotten him this far. Harry was the manager of the club, though, and he knew he couldn't just go up and say hello. There was a line and you didn't cross it. So instead, Liam just sat on the bench outside the changing rooms and waited for the kit to be put out and his boots to be brought up. It would be at least an hour until most of the first-team players would turn up, and Liam was changed and sitting back on the bench by the time the players started to file in. Scottish centre-forward Ryan McCoughlan was the first. Ryan had won the Golden Boot last year as top scorer in the Second Division. He was thirty now and this was his thirteenth year as a professional footballer. He had scored goals his whole career. Last season had been a life-changer for Ryan. He had finally managed to quit drinking, and he had reconciled with his wife. He had now moved out of his apartnment and was now living at home again. Harry had been instrumental in Ryan's change of fortune. In a season of highs for Harry, Ryan getting his life back on track had been the highest. Ryan had been on a downward spiral with alcohol for years, and those demons might have cost him his life had he not faced them down.

"Hey partner," said Ryan as he shook Liam by the hand. Liam and Ryan played up front together and had formed a deadly partnership.

"Hey Ryan."

Ryan looked tanned and healthy. He had clearly enjoyed his summer. "Have you grown? You look taller?" asked Ryan.

Liam just shrugged; his mum had been saying the same thing.

"I forget you're still a wee laddie. You're nearer Darren's age than mine! You know he wanted a Clifton Rangers top with your name on it. My own son. In the end I bribed him with a new game for his Nintendo."

Liam laughed awkwardly as Ryan went on his way.

The players were arriving thick and fast by now and it wasn't long before Liam saw Jason arriving.

"Where were you this morning, Blackie?" asked Liam.

Jason fished in his pocket then dangled a set of keys, a huge grin on his face. "I'm a First Division player now, can't be begging lifts off Johnny mate."

They both laughed and shook hands. Jason told Liam every detail of his new purchase, from engine size to the upholstery, all in his thick West Country drawl. Even though he had worked in his Uncle Gary's garage for more than a year, Liam still knew nothing about cars and had no interest. But he nodded at all the right places and made all the right noises. A bit like his mum did when he talked about football.

A few players walked past as they spoke, and the players all exchanged handshakes and hellos with Liam. When a shellsuit-clad Greg strode up, he stayed and joined in the conversation and it wasn't long before they were telling stories from their youth team days. Everyone who went past seemed to have a Spanish suntan and looked slightly portlier than they had at the end of the season. The common understanding was that preseason was for getting rid of the excesses of the summer. No-one exercised in the summer, and they all took the chance to enjoy the break. The coaches might moan a bit at the first weigh-in, but nobody was too bothered.

"Out the way runt!" growled a hard-faced man, who barged into Liam as he walked past. He had a face that looked like it had been carved out of wood and there was an intimidating bite to his voice. This was Reg Varney, Clifton Rangers' self-proclaimed hard man. Liam gulped. *Not again*, he thought. Then a smile appeared on Reg's face and he gave Liam a 'friendly' jab in the arm. "Only joking kid, I've got your back! Look on your face though! Priceless!"

Liam gave a smile of relief. Reg had made his and Jason's lives unbearable when they had first got into the first team. But now everyone in football knew that if you messed with Liam, then you would have to deal with Reg.

While Jason and the others got changed for training, Liam stood at the bottom of the stairs to the changing rooms and watched the youth team play piggy. To play, you form a circle and one player,the piggy, went in the middle. Then the other players passed the ball around the outside while the piggy in the middle tried to get the ball. To get in the youth team at a First Division club you had to be technically good, and all these boys would have been the best player at their schools. It wasn't easy if you were stuck in the middle but great fun on the outside. Piggy in the middle was a good way of marking your territory; letting people know you deserved to be there. For the new YTS trainees, this was their first chance to impress. The main attraction of the game, though, was the chance to humiliate the player in the middle. If you could "nutmeg" them by getting the ball through their legs, that was good, but if you could call it first then that was the ultimate humiliation. "Nuts!" would come the call, then the ball would be passed between the player's legs and the whole game would stop while everyone, except the piggy, jumped around like excited puppies. You had to be careful, though. Liam had played it with the first team once. Bradley 'Chippy' Carpenter, Rangers' talented ex-England international midfielder, had nutmegged Reg after calling it. No-one celebrated. The next time Chippy got the ball, Reg nearly cut him in half with a Reggie special, Reggie was known for his ferocious slide tackles. He then stood over Chippy's prone body, growling. They had played piggy only the once.

Liam stood watching the young players, jealous of the banter and camaraderie. He hadn't been in the youth team long before he was pulled into the first team squad, and he felt like he had somehow missed out - not fully aware that every one of the youth team wished they could follow the same path as him.

Jason appeared at his shoulder, "Looks like fun, eh mate? Shall we?"

Liam looked at Jason then at the game then back at Jason. "Be rude not to!"

"Halesy, you coming?" called Jason to Greg Hales, who was over by the lunch hall having just poured himself a cup of tea. Greg chucked the tea on the floor and ran over laughing, just as Jason and Liam joined the circle.

"Last one's piggy mate! You know the rules," said Jason, directing a crestfallen Greg to the middle of the circle.

Chapter Four

The game of piggy was brought to a premature end by Doug Clemance, the first team assistant manager, calling the first team into the changing room. Doug was a huge man with hands like shovels. It was no surprise that he had been a goalkeeper as a player, and a fine one at that. Everyone took their customary seats. Doug and Harry entered the changing room and closed the door behind them. Alex Kempster, the youth team coach, was also with them.

"Morning gents," began Harry. He was dressed in a suit and as immaculate as ever. He had salt-and-pepper hair, but still looked fit enough to play. "It's great to be back, not just to training, but to the First Division. Never felt right, this great club being out of it. I'm sure you've read the papers and, if not, I know you've seen the odds in the bookies!"

At this there were a few wry glances and smiles amongst the players.

"No-one's giving us a chance, everyone has us down for an immediate return to the Second Division," Harry continued. "Well, they can stick their predictions. I've every faith in the players in this room. So, there'll be no new players, other than Halesy joining us from the youth team. You'll all get a chance to prove yourselves in this division. Don't waste it."

A few players banged their hands on the benches in support at this, and Jason nudged Greg in the ribs.

"We do, though, have another promotion from the youth team," Harry said. "From today, Alex Kempster will be helping Doug with training. I know you all know Alex, and I expect you to give him the same respect you've given Doug and me. He's a legend at this club, and just the sort of character we need."

Again, benches were hit in support. Liam beamed at this news; Alex was another person who had played a big part in his progress from the youth team. It now meant that, in Harry and Alex, they had two members of the Rangers' European Cup winning side of '76 on the coaching staff.

"I've put my faith in every one of you in this room," Harry continued. "We have more than enough ability and know how in this changing room to not just stay up, but to prove a few people wrong. They can write us off all they want. We are Clifton Rangers, and we are going to shove their predictions back down their throats. From today, everything we do is towards that goal. Let's get our heads straight and our minds right. Blood, toil, tears and sweat boys, blood, toil, tears and sweat. Now get out there and let's start as we mean to go on!"

The players rose as one. It was like a match day not a training day. Players slapping each other on the back. Shouts of, "Come on Rangers!" and, "Let's do this lads!" filled the air and could be heard as the first team players disappeared out past the trees towards the first team training area. Alex was with them, but Doug waited behind for a moment.

"That's good going, day one and you've already thrown in a Churchill quote. I like the way you didn't mention that you *couldn't* bring anyone in even if you wanted to," remarked Doug.

"Yeah, don't think they need to know that the Chairman's a tight son of a bitch, do they?"

13

Chapter Five

Being a top-level footballer is the dream of billions of children all over the world. The reality is pretty much as good as the dream. With one exception... preseason training.

Imagine being taken to your absolute limit. You can't catch your breath. You feel like you are going to throw up. Every muscle aches. Your brain screams at you to stop. All the time, an angry giant with huge hands screams at you to do one more lap, one more circuit, one more hill, one more press-up, one more sit-up, one more, one more. Then you look around you and you know that, if you want to make the team, you must be better than the person next to you. Quicker, stronger, more focused. The whole time you are acutely aware that this is your dream. That you are so close you can touch it.

"Faster! Anyone who is over twelve minutes will do the run again. Three laps to go," the booming voice of Doug announced. Or Field Marshall Clemence as the players had named him. Though not in earshot obviously. The response, though, was unusual. Up and down the country in similar situations, there are many who rebel. Hold a bit back, save a bit in the tank. But not at Clifton. This team had been through a lot together, and if one started to fall behind, they all pulled them back in again. The cliques at the club had long been expelled, this was a team in every sense of the word.

Later, in the changing room, it was like a scene from a war movie. There were bodies everywhere. Some stretched out fully across the floor, others doubled over on the benches that surrounded the room. Bin bags littered the floor, all glistening in sweat. This was common in preseason training as players wore them under their kit to sweat out the excess pounds.

"Someone turn on the showers," said Chippy, "give 'em a chance to warm up."

"Can't move mate," came the reply from Jason.

"Me neither," said Liam.

The training kit was a light blue, but everyone's kit was a dark blue and a few pounds heavier from perspiration.

"Who remembers their first preseason?" asked Reg.

"I try not to," replied Jimmy Mimms, the team's goalkeeper.

"The first one's the worst! I was actually ill I was so run down."

"Unlike you to catch something!" quipped Reg, throwing a boot at Jimmy.

Everyone's laughter turned to a cheer as Jimmy caught the boot and held it up like he had just saved a penalty.

Upstairs, Harry could hear the banter from the changing room. He knew that the team's togetherness could be crucial to the team's season. They were woefully undermanned. He had just seen the squad lists for the other First Division clubs. There wasn't a squad of less than twenty and the depth of experience was ridiculous. Tottenford had twenty-three full internationals in their squad. Clifton Rangers had sixteen professionals in total, and three of them were still teenagers. In the summer, Harry had tried on numerous occasions to contact David Salow, the club Chairman, to discuss transfer targets, but he hadn't received a reply. Then, two days before the start of preseason, he had received an email from Mr Salow's secretary telling him that Mr Salow considered the present squad to be adequate and no funds would be made available for additional players. Meanwhile, David Salow's business had recorded record profits for the third consecutive year.

Not for the first time, Harry wondered if he should just cut his losses and walk away. He was financially very well off. He had invested his money from football well, and had some success investing in the stock market. Right now, his own stock was extremely high. He had guided a relegation-threatened Clifton Rangers to promotion to the First Division in just two years. On a non-existent budget. He knew that there would be no shortage of interest if he did want to move on. But… this was Clifton Rangers, his team, Bill Jameson's team. Bill had been his manager when Harry was at the club as a player. It was Bill who had put the club on the map, taking them from the Third Division to the First Division title and then that glorious night in 1976 when they were crowned Champions of Europe. To walk away now would feel like betrayal. He had to take it as far as he could. Even if it meant a few more grey hairs. Besides, he had a long game in place. But he had to keep it under his hat for a while yet.

Chapter Six

When you only have sixteen players, then preseason matches can be nerve wracking. A fact that Harry had quickly discovered. With every tumble and every challenge, Harry held his breath, hoping that his player was okay. Luckily, other than a few minor knocks and strains, they had managed to get out to the other side pretty much intact. Results had been up and down, but preseason was ultimately a success because the whole squad was match fit and ready for the start of the season. Then there was Liam.

First, he had clearly grown a couple of inches and now filled his frame well. In the past, he had still been carrying a little puppy fat, but not anymore. He no longer looked like a boy in a man's game. He also seemed to have added a couple of yards of extra pace. Add that to his undoubted prodigious talent and you had... well, what you had didn't come along too often. The other players knew it too. Every player's first option of who to pass to seemed to be Liam. Players always know. If the club was going to stay in the First Division, then they had to get the most out of him.

Liam also had a couple of new tricks in his arsenal. Firstly, he had worked out a signal with Chippy. When Liam was on the halfway line he would start to move back to his own goal when Chippy had the ball, as if he wanted the ball passed to his feet. He would then tap his chest with the palm of his hand before quickly spinning and sprinting towards the opponent's goal. Thanks to the signal, Chippy would have already played the ball into the space for Liam to run onto. With his extra pace and the fact that he couldn't be offside as he had started in his own half, Liam would be clean through on goal. It had worked several times in the preseason matches.

Then there was the freekick they had concocted in training. When any team gets a freekick just outside the penalty area, the keeper's job is to line up the wall. To do that he moves behind the wall to one of the goal posts and lines up his defender on the edge of the wall, with the ball and then the post. The idea being that the wall blocks half the goal. He then goes and stands in the other half; the half he is expected to protect. The trick Liam and Chippy had worked out was that when the referee blew the whistle for the freekick to be taken, Chippy would pick up the ball and move it a yard to the side. The goalkeeper would then run back to the other post to line up the wall again. As he was running back to the post, Liam would step up and shoot to the other corner, on the side the keeper should have been protecting and had just vacated. They had scored twice in preseason doing it and so had saved it for the new season. Technically, the referee should have blown for a freekick for handball against Chippy, but they hadn't so far.

All in all, the players and staff were united in their optimism for the new season. Secretly, Harry just hoped for a season without too much drama.

He wasn't to get his wish.

Chapter Seven

There were only a couple of hours until the opening game of the season and Liam didn't know what to do with himself. He was driving his mum mad.

"Liam, babe, if you check your phone one more time I'm going to scream!"

Liam ignored his mum; Lisa was supposed to have called. He checked the volume on his phone again. It was still on its highest level. He considered ringing his phone from the house phone just to check that he really was getting a signal, even though he clearly had three bars. As much as he hated using the phone, he was desperate to talk to her. They had promised each other that they were going to make a go of it on the day she left, but it had been so rushed. They hadn't even been on an official date, and although Liam thought they were boyfriend and girlfriend, he wasn't entirely certain. Netfield, the city where Lisa's university was situated, was miles away, so the phone was the only way they could keep in touch. And she was late calling him. This was a familiar pattern. He had training and matches, she had lectures and assignments. Their schedules never seemed to align.

Liam dropped onto the sofa, pained. He was supposed to be preparing himself for his debut in the First Division and all he could think about was whether his bloody phone was working. He was going to have to leave in a moment and the club rule was no phones before or during the game.

"Will you stop moping around, haven't you got a game today?"

"How can you ask me that? It's the First Division. You do know what a big deal that is, don't you?"

"Still, not as steady as working at Gary's garage, is it? You could have been Boss there one day."

"Mum, I'm playing for Clifton Rangers, I'll be on Match of the Day tonight. You're unbelievable. As if I'm going to give that up to be some skivvy for Uncle Gary."

"Well, if you don't clean your room, you won't be going anywhere. I mean it Liam, it's a pigsty in there, babe."

"Oh mum… Can't I do it tomorrow? I really do need to get going. Blackie's picking me up in a minute, I said I'd meet him downstairs. You still coming? I'll leave a ticket at reception if you are."

"Yeah, course I am babe, wouldn't miss it for the world'" she said, even though Liam knew it was a lie. "It's good it's on the TV though, cos then when it starts getting cold it don't matter if I miss the odd game."

"Unbelievable!" sighed Liam as he grabbed his bag and went to leave, checking his phone one more time as he did so.

Chapter Eight

Liam had to listen to Jason tell him all about his car for the whole journey, but he was glad of the distraction. By the time they pulled up in the car park and got out the car, Lisa was at the back of his mind, as the reality of the day suddenly surrounded him. Today he was going to be a First Division player. For *his* Clifton Rangers. There was something different about the day, Liam and Jason could both sense it as they walked through reception and made their way to the changing rooms. The whole place was alive. It was truly a momentous day for the club, and you could see that everyone had made a special effort. Suits were pressed, glass was polished, smiles were stuck firmly in place. There were still a couple of hours until kick-off, but there was already a sense of urgency. The opponents were Skelton Forest. Skelton was a large industrial town pretty much as far to the north of England as you can get. They had been in the First Division for twenty-seven consecutive years and were expected to finish in the top half this season. Everyone was expecting a Skelton victory.

When Liam and Jason entered the changing room, the first thing they did was look at the huge whiteboard with a football pitch marked out in tape on it. The names of the players in the starting eleven were written in the positions they would play. Even though they expected it, they were still relieved to see the name Blackie at number six and Liam at number ten. They didn't say anything but looked at each other with an excited smile. They were the first ones there, but the changing room was already set up. The shirts were hung on the pegs and the table was full of a variety of items such as oils, rolls of tape, gum, Haribo sweets and smelling salts. They both grabbed a couple of handfuls of sweets before Johnny could see them and put their bags under their pegs.

"You see Halesy's on the bench," said Liam.

"Jesus Liam, it's only two years since we were all in the youth team together. Now look at us, mate."

"I know, Blackie. Honestly, I'm not sure I can do this. I'm not ready for this. A First Division footballer. I was playing park football for the Beer-Belly Eleven two years ago."

Before Jason could answer, the door swung open and e a few of the other players came into the room.

"Too late now, mate," said Jason, still smiling and picking up a couple more Haribo cola bottles.

Before long, everyone was there, and some of the early preparations had started. A few players were getting their legs massaged, others were out on the pitch making sure they had the right footwear for the game while a few sat quietly, mentally going through the game in their head. There was the normal sympathy and words of comfort given to the lads who hadn't made the team. But with such a small squad, they knew they would get their chance at some stage and, as a result, they didn't sulk and tried to show everyone that they were still supporting the team. One thing was for sure; Ken had done a fantastic job on the pitch. Despite the long, hot summer the grass was lush and green and huge circles had been mowed into it.

Time seemed to fly by, and the players were soon out on the pitch doing the warmup. The fans had already started to turn up and the Forest end was full, with a fleet of coaches having brought the supporters all the way down from Skelton that morning. Liam watched the Skelton players doing their warmup. They seemed so confident, so self-assured that his doubts returned. He must have undone and done up his laces ten times during the warmup and adjusted his shinpads a further twelve. He just didn't feel comfortable and, when the Clifton players got the balls out, Liam's touch felt clumsy and his passing lacked its usual crispness.

Back in the changing room, Doug went over the set pieces and then handed over to Harry. Liam could barely focus on what Harry was saying, he felt like he was in a dream almost looking in from outside. The bell rang and they made their way out onto the pitch.

***

"Come on boys, bleeding wake up!" yelled Terry Johns, Clifton's veteran centre-half, "We're getting mullered here!"

And he was right, it was 1-0 to Skelton but it could have been five. Liam's form from the warmup had continued, but he was no worse than another six or seven Clifton players. Everything was reactionary. The Skelton players would pass the ball, then the Clifton players would move, always one step behind. Liam felt like he had been chasing shadows for half an hour.

The second goal was more of the same. Another long Skelton passing move finished with a neat, chipped finish over Jimmy Mimms. Not one Clifton player had got anywhere near any of the Skelton players. When the half-time whistle went, the Clifton players were both relieved and lucky to still only be losing 2-0. The Skelton fans sang "Can we play you every week?" as the players left the field and made their way up the tunnel. The Clifton fans had been surprisingly quiet all afternoon, almost as if they too were unsure that they belonged in the First Division.

Reggie kicked over the water bottles and let out a primal scream as he entered the changing room. He punched the wall, bloodying his knuckles. Terry Johns, the Clifton veteran defender, also looked like he wanted to punch something. The size of him, if he punched the wall, he might bring it down. Everyone else just flopped into their spaces in silence, and tried to avoid catching the eye of Terry or Reggie. Liam wasn't sure if he was going to cry or throw up.

"Right, everyone settle down," said Harry as he made eye contact with Reg and Terry. "What did you think? You were just going to turn up and it would just happen for you? These are proper players. You've got to earn the right to play. Reggie, Terry, we need that aggression on the pitch. Get amongst them, let's see how they like a few challenges. You're all showing them too much respect. Liam and Chippy, you look like you want to get their autographs out there. I wouldn't have any one of their midfield over you two, but you look like you're apologising for being here. Get hold of the ball make them do the chasing a bit. I don't know how, but we're still in this. I don't care about the result now. I just want to see some fight; I want you to show me that I was right to believe in you."

Liam tried to get himself going, but he couldn't seem to convince himself that Harry was right. He felt numb. The team talk ended. The players lined up and made their way back on to the pitch. Again, the crowd's response was muted, and the Forest fans could clearly be heard above those supporting Clifton. Harry looked around. "Not like in our day, eh Alex," he remarked to Alex Kempster, his old teammate from the Clifton glory days.

"Not at all H, I can remember them carrying us through games in those days, they were like an extra man to us."

"We could do with an extra man today," said Harry.

As they lined up for the second half, a lot of the motivational calls of the players were aimed at Liam. They could tell he was off the pace of the game, but they knew that if anyone could make a difference, it was him. Unfortunately, he didn't have their faith.

The start of the second half was an improvement. Defensively, led by Terry and Reggie, Clifton were more aggressive. Skelton were no longer having it their own way, and everyone could see that they weren't enjoying it quite so much. One tackle by Reggie even got a bit of a reaction from the crowd. But offensively they were non-existent. Ryan was a goalscorer, but he relied on others to create his chances. He wasn't the type of player to create something out of nothing. That was what Liam did. Chippy was normally the team's other chance creator, but he was overrun in midfield and saw little of the ball. A fully functioning Liam made everyone around him play better.

Whenever Liam had got the ball, he had looked to pass it on as quickly as possible, not wanting to make a mistake. About ten minutes into the second half, he went to do the same again. But the Skelton midfielder blocked the intended pass to Chippy so instead, Liam was forced to take a touch and turn, just about managing to avoid a couple of challenges. He was now facing the Skelton goal. Again, he looked to get rid of the ball. This time to Scott Fulling, the Rangers' right winger. But again, he couldn't quite find a gap. So instead, he knocked the ball past the next Skelton midfielder and accelerated into the space. The Skelton players almost looked confused; this was not in the script. Liam was working on instinct. The next Skelton player tried to tackle him, but Liam had seen him coming and slipped past him with no real effort. He was now running directly at the centre of Skelton's defence. Now the crowd were involved, as if someone had turned on a switch. Liam felt it as he surged forward. Other than the last two defenders and goalkeeper, it was like everyone had been frozen in time; helpless to do anything other than watch. Even Ryan hadn't made a run. Caught up in the moment, he seemed transfixed on what Liam was going to do next. All eyes were on the Clifton number ten. He pulled his leg back as if he was going to shoot. The two defenders panicked and slid in to block the shot. But Liam wasn't shooting. Instead, he put his left foot on top of the ball and dragged it away from the sliding defenders. He then switched feet, using his right foot to drag it back towards the goal and past the startled, prone defenders. He had put himself clean though on goal by performing a pirouette. As the keeper rushed out, Liam sidestepped him almost without thinking. He then took an extra touch to steady himself before sliding the ball into the empty net. Only when the ball hit the back of the net, did he fully comprehend what he had just done. The crowd was silent. Even his own teammates took a second to process what they had just seen. Then the whole stadium erupted. The noise was deafening and a still-stunned Liam was knocked to the floor and disappeared under a sea of celebrating teammates.

The players lined up ready for Skelton to take kick off. The ground was alive with noise, and the Clifton players exchanged nods of determination. Liam had shown them they belonged, now they had to prove it. The rest of the game was a frenzy of attacking football from Clifton. First, Ryan curled a great effort onto the crossbar following a clever pass by Liam. Then Liam and Chippy almost combined with their secret signal, only a desperate lunge from the Skelton keeper preventing Liam from scoring. All the action was at the Skelton Forest end. But the equaliser refused to come.

Liam looked up at the clock. They were into stoppage time. His nerves were now completely behind him, and he was running the game. Everything seemed to go through him and everything he tried seemed to come off. Skelton had no answers, and their defending had become more and more desperate. Liam made one last forward run. Ryan had chased down a clearance and managed to pass the ball off to Chippy on the left-hand side of the penalty area. Chippy immediately transferred it across to the oncoming Liam. Without breaking stride, Liam struck the ball perfectly. It was a sweet connection and the ball arrowed towards the top corner of the goal. The crowd rose in celebration. Liam watched the ball as it travelled as if in slow motion. A cheer frozen in his throat. Out of nowhere came the very fingertips of the Skelton goalkeeper to touch the ball a fraction higher on to the face of the crossbar. The crossbar was still shaking as the referee blew the final whistle. Liam had been an inch away from a spectacular equaliser. Several Clifton players fell to their knees, while the Skelton players ran to congratulate their goalkeeper.

Eventually, the dejected Clifton players began to leave the field. No reward for their Herculean second-half showing. Then it began. It started as a murmur and rose and rose to a breathtaking crescendo. Not a single fan had left the ground. Not a single fan remained in their seat. Not a single fan failed to add their voice. As one they rose, cheered and clapped *their* Clifton Rangers. Liam was not the only player to have a lump in his throat.

Harry stood at the edge of the tunnel.

"Off you go," he said pointing them back out onto the pitch.

The appreciative Clifton players carried their exhausted bodies around the pitch, returning the applause of the fans. The coaching staff, subs and even the unused players followed, thanking the fans for their support.

Harry and Alex looked around them. It was good to be back.

Chapter Nine

The changing room was a strange place to be after the game. Harry had told them to take the second-half performance as a benchmark and look to build on it for the next game. The fact was, though, that they had lost. Not one of the team would sleep well that night, and wives and families would not be looking forward to them coming home. Defeats remained with sportsmen and sportswomen for a long time and they were never good company following one. Liam and Jason went up to the players' lounge after the game as that was what was expected of them but, as soon as they could, they made their excuses and left. Even footballers don't want to be around footballers after a loss.

When they got into reception and looked outside, it was bedlam. There were photographers and press everywhere and there must have been a couple of hundred fans waiting outside the entrance.

"What's going on?" Liam asked the security guard.

"What d'you think? They're waiting for you," he replied.

Liam had to put his hands over his eyes to protect them from the flashes of the cameras and Jason had to be careful not to get crushed as the fans rushed forwards. The security guard stepped outside with them and helped them get to Blackie's car. All the while, members of the press were throwing questions at Liam about the game. There was no way Liam could have managed to sign one programme, it was just too crazy. It took them about five minutes to crawl through the crowd and out the gate. Neither of them said a word until they got to Liam's flat.

"What was that all about?" said Liam finally.

"You just don't get it, do you? It's like a secret that only you don't know mate. Except, it's *not* a secret anymore."

Liam just looked at him, confused.

"Liam you're good, bloody good. Brilliant even. The best player we have by a mile. You're the only one who doesn't know it. Why do you think everyone wants to be on your team in training? Cos if we're against you, we're all scared you're gonna show us up! And then today Liam, against international players, as an eighteen-year-old, on your First Division debut, you scored the best goal I've ever seen. You can bet by tomorrow everyone in the country will know your name after that goal, mate. This is just the beginning. You think that was mad outside the ground today? Wait until Match of the Day tonight!"

Liam had no words. He waved Jason away, and made his way up the stairs to his flat. On the way, he took his phone out his pocket and turned it on. He turned the key in the door just as the phone finished starting up. Seven missed calls. Liam tried to call Lisa back, but it just rang out. *Perfect,* thought Liam.

"Liam, is that you, babe?"

"Yeah mum."

"Go clean your room, babe, dinner'll be ready soon."

Chapter Ten

The fixtures for Clifton were not kind. The next four games were all against sides expected to finish in the top half of the league. Harry felt that they played well in all four games and yet they had managed to lose all four.

It was Thursday night. The stadium was deserted. He was sitting alone in his office, which overlooked the pitch. Every game had been close, all being decided by one or two goals. Once again, luck just wasn't on their side. Part of the problem was the familiar old story of the smaller team not seeming to get the big decisions. Two of the games had contentious penalty decisions, and Harry was certain that Liam should have had a couple given in his favour. If he had more players in his squad he could throw in some fresh legs, but he knew that the starting eleven was his best team. He didn't think there was much wrong. What *was* worrying was that there was an anxiety that had crept into the team's game. Defensively, they were making rash decisions. In attack, they either snatched at their chances or delayed too long trying to be too precise.

The only player who had looked unaffected was Liam. He had scored all of Clifton's goals so far. With three goals in five games, he was getting rave reviews. He was clearly suited to this level of football. It was less crash, bang, wallop and more tactical and technical. Already, there were questions as to whether Clifton were going to be able to keep hold of him. Harry knew that if they were going to keep him, then they were going to have to start winning matches, and soon.

Harry had been racking his brains about what to do. In times like these, he always thought back to his time under Bill Jameson. What would Bill do? What had Bill done? Then it came to him. It was a long shot, but what did he have to lose? He would have a word with Alex tomorrow and put the wheels in motion.

It wasn't like things were about to get any easier. Saturday they were away.

At Tottenford.

Chapter Eleven

Liam hated him. He didn't know him, but he hated him. Dean Beadle had just scored his second goal and was standing in front of the Clifton Rangers fans posing like some sort of gladiator. "This is my house!" he was shouting over and over at the Clifton away support, basking in their abuse.

The fact that no-one on Beadle's team was celebrating with him said something about his character. Reggie ran over and grabbed him by the shirt to drag him away from the Clifton away fans. A scuffle ensued. As the opposing teams were pulled apart, Beadle just jogged back to his own half, laughing out loud with a huge grin on his face. Not even caring when he was booked by the referee for inciting the away support. As he went past Liam, he said, "That's how you do it sunshine. You can have this lesson for free."

Liam had an almost overwhelming urge to punch him, but he knew that's what Beadle wanted. Over his short career, Dean Beadle had probably been responsible for more players getting sent off than any other player. He just had this knack for getting under people's skin. The problem was, he was good. And he knew it. He was less than a year older than Liam but had been playing in the First Division for three years now. Last year he was top scorer, and had won the PFA Young player of the year. The fans loved him, and he was the golden boy of English football. But he was probably the most disliked man within football. The rumour was that Tottenford had bought his family a house when he was still fourteen. It was a fact that his Dad was given a well-paid job by the club. Everyone had known Tottenford had a star in the making, and Beadle had enjoyed all the privileges of playing for one of the biggest teams in the world. He was an extraordinarily rich young man before he had even kicked a ball for the first team.

There had been a gulf in class between the two teams that day. The Tottenford side was like a who's who of international football. They had two top-class players for every position and three or four world-class talents. Dean Beadle was one of them.

This was the first time that the Clifton Rangers team had looked out of their depth. They were never in the game. The final score was 4-0 and it was a dejected team that left the field and made its way back into the changing room. Harry didn't know what to say to them. They were giving him everything, but things were snowballing. With every loss, the team's confidence was getting lower and lower. With low confidence came more mistakes, more missed chances. That was now six straight losses. Harry decided he was going to have to put his plan into action. The next game was midweek, away to Kirkby, who were in sixth place.

His thoughts were interrupted by the changing room door being flung open. Everyone looked up to see the cause of the interruption. Dean Beadle stood in the doorway with an arrogant grin on his face.

"Why so sad lads? You're only one game away from being record breakers!" he said, a smirk on his face.

Terry Johns stood up and stepped menacingly towards him. Beadle backed away, his hands up in mock apology, not so brave without a referee to protect him. Terry slammed the door shut behind Beadle, almost taking it off its hinges.

"Tosser," said Reggie. "What's he going on about? Record breakers?"

"Didn't you know Reggie?" said Terry, "We just tied the record for the worst start. If we lose Wednesday, we'll officially be the worst team in First Division history!"

Great, thought Harry, *that's going to help our confidence.*

Chapter Twelve

On Monday, at training, the surprise news that they were going to be staying overnight in Kirkby before Wednesday's game was delivered. It was a surprise as everyone knew how miserly the Chairman was. They had never stayed overnight anywhere before. Even the coach the team travelled in was budget. No-one knew it was Harry who was paying. They checked into a plush hotel on the outskirts of Kirkby and were even able to train at a local sports centre. After training, most the players went back to their rooms to watch TV or sleep. A few of them found the hotel's pool table and had a few games. The mood was subdued after Saturday's loss. Dinner was set for 6.30pm and was eaten almost in silence.

Harry stood up when everyone had finished. "Right lads, me and Doug have got a few things we need to get sorted for tomorrow, so Alex is going to take you for a bit of a walk. Kirkby's a beautiful old town, I'm sure you'll enjoy it. We've a bit of lunch laid on for 12.00 tomorrow which means you can get a lie in. See you all here at 11.45 tomorrow. Don't be late."

Harry asked Ryan to stay behind for a moment.

You could tell the players weren't too thrilled about the idea of a walk around Kirby. Alex could hear a few moans as they came out of the hotel about wanting to rest up in their rooms. The walk took them across a field, and again Alex heard moaning about getting their trainers and tracksuit bottoms dirty. On the other side of the field was a steep incline and Alex heard complaining about having to walk up it. At the top was a small little village with a church, a convenience store and a pub called the White Horse. Alex heard a few surprised voices as he turned into the car park and made his way up to the door of the pub. They weren't moaning anymore.

"What's going on Alex?" asked Chippy.

"Let's call it a bit of team bonding," came the reply.

It was a small country pub with a thatched roof and an inglenook fireplace. The floor was wooden, and beams ran across the ceiling. Luckily, there were a few tables that had been pushed together with benches around them so all the players could sit together. Alex got the drinks in.

"Fifteen pints of bitter and two orange juices please, landlord,"

The landlord had a thick bushy beard that was in stark contrast to the hairless crown of his head. His eyes lit up at the large order. He was clearly happy for the unexpected business, even though Kirkby memorabilia could be seen all round the bar area.

"Coming right up. Take a seat I'll bring them over."

Liam and Ryan took the orange juices as the only teetotallers in the squad. The rest of the team sipped at their beers as they sat around the table, unsure of how to act. In the old days it was a lot more liberal, and players were often seen out on the town the night before a game. The recent influx of foreign players and coaches had meant that this was changing. Most clubs now had a fourty-eight hour, no-alcohol-before-a-game rule. There were still a few players in England who were known to break these rules, but the thought was that if they were performing on the pitch then the clubs would turn a blind eye. Not always in the best interests of the player.

"Right, who wants another?" Alex had finished his drink and was already standing and on his way to the bar. "Drinks are on the club!"

In his hand, Alex waved the club credit card.

"Count me in!" said Jimmy Mimms.

Players were now sinking their drinks ready for their second.

"Won't you get in trouble, Alex?" asked Liam as he joined Alex at the bar.

"What they don't know won't hurt them," Alex replied with a wink.

As the evening progressed and the players got more and more lubricated, things got a lot more relaxed. The banter was flying around, and everyone was sharing stories. Laughter filled the pub. Even though they weren't drinking, Ryan and Liam were both caught up in the mood and were as loud and boisterous as everyone else.

"Reg, your face on Saturday when that arrogant sod was celebrating in front of our fans. I thought you were going to end him!" said Greg Hales with a laugh.

"I thought about throwing him over the fence for our fans to do the job for me. All I know is, he's lucky he got away when Terry went for him. There would have been nothing left if Terry had got his hands on him!" said Reggie.

"We've still got them to play at home yet," the deep voice of Terry said.

Everyone at the table collapsed into laughter.

"Anyone fancy a bit of Karaoke?"

The players all looked up to see Alex holding a karaoke machine and a couple of microphones.

"Where d'you get that from?" asked Jason.

"Don't worry about that, who's first up?" said Alex.

In the end, Alex started them off. He had a half-decent voice and his rendition of "Sweet Caroline" was more than passable. By the time he got to the second chorus, everyone was singing along and banging on the table at the appropriate time.

Next, Greg Hales surprised the group with an excellent Elvis impression, including the hip movements. But that was not the highlight.

Bryan Adams had been number one for seventeen weeks with a song from the film Robin Hood. It was called "Everything I Do" and it was fair to say the English population was beginning to get a little fed up with it. It seemed to constantly be on the radio and was almost impossible to escape. It was Jason "Blackie" Blackmore who, to many groans, announced that this was the song he was going to sing. He may not have hit any of the notes - he was to claim later that he hit all the notes just not necessarily in the right order - but anyone who was fortunate enough to have seen it would agree that Bryan Adams himself would not have been as entertaining. You certainly could not have accused Jason of not putting his all into it. He seemed almost transported to a stadium gig or festival. Some of the faces he pulled had the Clifton squad literally struggling to breathe they were laughing so much. His dancing was even worse. Much to Liam's embarrassment, and everyone else's delight, Jason not only dedicated the song to Liam, but also directed the whole performance at him, gazing into Liam's eyes as if he was Maid Marion to Jason's Robin Hood. Even Liam couldn't keep a straight face, finding it as hysterical as everyone else, if a little

33

disturbing. The roar of approval at the end almost took the thatched roof straight off the pub.

When the players eventually crawled back into the hotel in the early hours, their efforts at being quiet were nearly as funny as Jason's performance.

"Shhhhh!" exclaimed Terry to Chippy. His shushing being much louder than the giggling coming from the inebriated Chippy. Players were struggling to open doors. Falling up the stairs. Breaking into laughter at the smallest provocation. At one point, there was even a few choruses of "Everything I do," which were soon silenced by more loud shushing and laughter.

In room twenty-three, listening at the door, Harry and Doug were also trying to not make too much noise.

"Hope you know what you're doing Harry."

"Me too, Clem, me too," replied Harry.

Chapter Thirteen

Lunch was hilarious. It consisted of the players pretending they weren't hungover, while Harry and Doug pretended they didn't know anything about it.

"Not hungry, Jason?" asked Harry innocently as Jason turned his nose up at his lunch.

"Err, pre-match nerves Boss, never eat much on a game day." Muffled giggles rippled around the table.

"He's pining for Maid Marion," whispered Greg.

This time no one could keep the laughter in.

Even nursing hangovers, the mood was completely different to the meal the night before. All the players were in high spirits. Conversations were bouncing around the table and everyone was in high jinks, like a table of naughty schoolchildren. Harry and Doug shared a look. Just maybe...

The players were all relieved when Harry told them they should rest up in their rooms for the afternoon and they would meet in the lobby, ready to leave at 5.45pm. Harry asked Ryan to stay behind.

"How was it last night?" Harry asked.

"Boss, it was hilarious. I had a great night."

"Were you okay?"

"Yeah, I was good Boss, didn't need a drink to enjoy that! Cheers for the heads up yesterday, but I wouldn't have missed that for the world."

"Good to hear it. Okay, see you in the lobby later."

The afternoon passed without incident and the players were soon on the coach and on the way to the ground. Kirkby was one of those towns where it was like life had stood still. The high street still looked like you would imagine it had a hundred years ago. The road was cobbled, and the buildings made of stone. It revelled in its history. The atmosphere on the coach was electric, and the journey seemed to pass in no time.

When they arrived, there was a larger-than-usual press presence. It had been a slow week for news. Several of the national papers had targeted in on the worst team in history story.

The Globe had even run with the heading IS THIS THE WORST TEAM IN HISTORY? With a picture of the team underneath. The article was scathing. Harry had been given a tip-off from a friend in the Globe press office and so had arranged with the hotel to hide all their complimentary newspapers; worried that it would affect confidence even further.

The cameras exploded to life as the players exited the coach. You could almost see the confusion on the cameramen's faces, though. This was not what they expected. The players looked relaxed and without a care in the world. They did not look like a team at the bottom of the league, let alone a team that could make history that day. The players were laughing and joking as they stepped off the coach, seemingly oblivious to events around them. Harry rushed them through reception to the changing rooms in an attempt to avoid questions from the press and protect his players. All his efforts went up in smoke when they got to the changing room. Someone had cut out and stuck the back page of The Globe on the dressing room door. Harry readied himself for the response. He had prepared a speech already just in case, he even had a few Churchill quotes prepared to throw in.

"Don't know about worst team," said Terry as he stopped to look at the cutting. "But definitely the worst singers!"

He gave Jason a playful push, nearly sending him flying into the treatment table in the middle of the room. The whole team erupted in laughter again. A few stopped and read it, making jokes about what they read. Most seemed to just ignore it.

"Here, Ryan and Chippy, it says you two are has-beens. I thought you had to be something first before you could be a has-been?" said Jimmy Mimms.

Chippy scooped a warmup ball off the floor and threw it at him. Jimmy batted it away.

"Looks like they were right about you though, you couldn't catch a bus!" quipped Chippy.

One of the Kirkby officials poked his head around the door, he seemed to be wondering what the noise was as once again a huge roar of laughter echoed along the tunnel. He turned to another club official in the corridor and said, "They're mad this lot, don't they know they're bottom of the league?"

Harry didn't need to do a team talk. Instead, he read the cutting from start to finish, emphasising every negative word. He then slowly ripped into up into strips and dropped it in the bin.

"You know what to do."

Even before they kicked a ball, the players could feel it. As they lined up in position and waited for kick off, they knew they were going to win. Harry knew it, Doug knew it. Alex knew it. When you had played football for long enough, you just knew when it was your day. They were quicker in the tackle, faster in thought and movement. Kirkby never stood a chance. All the frustration of the previous six games was used to produce what Harry would later describe as the best performance he had ever been part of. Certainly, one of the most satisfying. The final score was 5-0, It could have been ten-nil. Ryan returned to form with a fine hattrick and Chippy and Liam got the other two. Liam was exemplary, but so was everyone else.

The Kirkby players, staff and supporters were stunned. This was not what they had been expecting. They were just as surprised to hear the raucous, out-of-tune rendition of "Everything I Do" that could be heard coming from the Clifton changing room long after the final whistle.

Chapter Fourteen

Liam's Day

There was no mid-week game, so the players were given Wednesday off. Liam slept late and didn't emerge from his bedroom until midday. Lisa was supposed to be ringing him that day, but when he checked his phone there were no missed calls. He thought about ringing her, but didn't want to seem desperate. Maybe he would call her that night if she hadn't rung by then. He set himself a deadline of 7:00pm, feeling that wouldn't make him seem so desperate.

"Why don't you just ring her, babe?"

"Who?"

"Yeah, right. I've never seen someone check their phone so much in my life. You've only been up a couple of hours and you must have checked it like a hundred times. And I know for a fact she's the only contact in your address book. She's probably doing the same thing. Give her a call."

"She was supposed to ring me," replied Liam giving up on the pretence. "And there are others in my address book!"

"It's a joke, babe, I know what she means to you. She's the first person I've ever known give football a run for its money. You even answered the phone when she rang during Match of the Day on Saturday!"

"Do you really think, I should ring her? I don't want to seem desperate," Liam asked.

"Some girls like the desperate type. But, seriously, if she's half the girl you seem to think she is, she'll love you giving her a call when she isn't expecting it."

Liam decided he had nothing to lose. He took his phone and went to his room to make the call. He still got embarrassed talking to a girl in front of his mum.

After about eight rings it went to Lisa's answerphone for the third time. Liam was a little relieved. Now the onus was back on her. She would see 3 MISSED CALLS and then ring him back… if she really was still interested.

38

Liam's mum went out shopping when she saw Liam come back into the living room, still checking his phone and with the same 'little boy lost' look on his face.

When she returned at about five, Liam was still sitting in the same spot as when she had left him. He now had his phone attached to the charging cable and hastily dropped it when he heard her come through the door.

"Shouldn't you be at the club rehearsing or something?" she tried.

"No, Harry has told us that we need to recuperate. He said to have a bath and an early night."

"Blinding, babe. Glad to see you do whatever Harry says. See I'm going to have a great night. Just the three of us."

"The three of us?"

"Yeah. Me, you and your bloody phone!"

Liam's mum started to run his bath for him at about quarter to seven. EastEnders was on at seven and the only miserable faces she wanted to see were those of the Mitchells and the Fowlers.

Liam even took his phone into the bathroom with him. When he had finished, he checked it again. Still nothing.

Liam was like every teenage boy up and down the country, it was amazing how much noise he could make just getting a drink from the kitchen. But it did mean his mum could hear that he had finished and was back in his bedroom. She finished watching EastEnders and then went to check on him.

"Bless him," she said as she opened the door.

There was Liam flat out on his bed, towel around his waist, his blonde mop of hair still damp from the bath. He was fast asleep. It was easy to forget that he was still her little boy. He may have been thrown into an adult world, but he was still her boy. All he seemed to do was play football and then come home. Outside of football, he seemed to have nothing. After much huffing and puffing she managed to manoeuvre him under the covers. She kissed him on his forehead. Turned out the light and left the room. *I hope she's not messing my little boy about*, she thought.

Back in the bathroom Liam's phone sat like a discarded toy. On the screen it said 7 MISSED CALLS. This, though, was soon replaced as the phone lit up once more; the word LISA filled the screen.

Lisa's Day

Lisa was up early again. She still hadn't got used to living in the university dorms. It was never quiet. It seemed like everyone had come to university to party. Half the girls in her dorm never went to the lectures. She got it, really. First time away from home. Letting loose. Chance to be a bit wild. But for Lisa, it was different. She knew what she wanted. And he wasn't here. She was also struggling with the course. Everything was theory, she couldn't keep up, and part of her didn't care. When she had applied for university, she had been living in a flat over the chemist in Clifton High Street. She and Liam weren't talking, and her dad was smothering her. When she looked back on it, she couldn't tell if she was running away from Liam or defying her father. She wasn't even sure she wanted to work in media anymore. She had been doing some media work at Clifton Rangers and had enjoyed it, that's why she had picked Media Studies. With hindsight, she now realised it was working at Clifton Rangers that she had enjoyed. That bloody club. Her whole life seemed to revolve around it. First as a child, sitting in the Chairman's box with her grandad, Alan Salow, the much-loved Chairman during Clifton's glory years. He had pumped much of the family's fortune into Clifton. It was his money that had renovated the whole stadium in the 70s, and it was him who had brought Bill Jameson to the club. Clifton Park - the house that Bill built. That's what they said, but Lisa knew differently. Clifton Rangers had also split her family apart. She was old enough to remember the blazing rows between her father and her grandad over the club, right up to her grandfather's dying days. Her dad had never understood it, never felt the connection. But to her, Clifton Rangers felt like part of her very being. And then, to top it all, she fell in love with a Clifton Rangers player. Liam Osborne. Her Liam. How she longed to be with him again. Chuck it all in and go home. Home to Clifton. Home to him.

She checked her watch. She had the urge to ring him, but it was too early. It was his day off, and she knew he needed his rest. Lisa knew her football. Players of Liam's age were usually in and out of the team. It was a way to protect them, stop them from burning out. But Clifton did not have that luxury. She had a lecture at nine, then a class at eleven, so she planned to give him a ring at lunch. Her days were planned around talking to him. Her worst days were the ones with no contact. All the doubts, the worry.

"Don't forget study group this afternoon Lisa," said Lorna. Lorna was pretty much Lisa's only friend at university. She was a mature student like Lisa. Mature! They were both only twenty but neither of them had gone straight to university from school, having chosen to live in the real world first for a while. It was only two years, but they felt a lifetime apart from the other students.

"Oh, God. I need to ring Liam."

"You do make me laugh. It'll be done by four! I'm sure he can wait!"

"I... I guess so."

Study group consisted of twelve students and one tutor. It seemed to go on forever. They had an assignment on the role of media in their own lives. Lisa didn't even understand the title. This study group was supposed to be for anyone who was finding the assignment difficult. It appeared to Lisa that, other than her and Lorna, everyone else understood it perfectly well. The rest of the group were honour students who just saw it as a way of getting more credit. At 5.00pm, they were finally finished. Lisa felt like the only thing she got out of the study group was a headache, and a few more doubts. Lisa hurried outside. She switched on her phone; phones were banned in study group. Her heart sank when she saw the three missed calls.

"You coming out for a drink at the Uni bar tonight?" asked Lorna as she joined her outside.

"No thanks Lorn, I've got a stinking headache and I really need to ring Liam."

"Okay, suit yourself. If you change your mind, give me a bell."

Lisa said she would and headed off to her dorm.

She stopped off at the campus shop to get a packet of paracetamol and a Pot Noodle on the way. Her dorm was in the student village and, by the time she got back to her room, it was nearly six. She knew Liam normally had his tea at about 6.00pm as his mum was a big EastEnders fan and never missed an episode. She decided to give him a ring at seven.

She ate her Pot Noodle, took her tablets and lay on her bed, going over her notes from study group. Trying to make some sense of them.

She must have nodded off as, when she checked her watch, it was nearly seven thirty. Liam! She quickly grabbed her phone.

"Pick it up, pick it up," she said to herself as the phone continued to ring. "*Please* pick it up, Liam."

After about ten tries she eventually gave up. Where could he be? It wasn't late. Even Liam didn't go to bed that early. What if he was out? What if he was with someone else? She had to force herself to stop thinking like that. What they had was special. They were in love, and they *would* be together.

One thing she did know was that she needed to get out of this room. It was dangerous, being alone with her thoughts. She dialled a number on her phone.

"Hi Lorn, you still want that drink?"

Chapter Fifteen

The convincing win against Kirkby had given the players the belief that they had been missing. Defensively, they were very solid, with Jason and Terry forming a great partnership. With Jason's pace and mobility alongside Terry's strength and organisational skills, it was a perfect match. From September through to November, the season went well for the club. In the thirteen games they played, they won six, drew four and lost three. They were out of the relegation places and had closed the gap on the teams above them. Everyone at the club was optimistic that they would soon begin to climb the table.

Almost everyone.

Liam's form had continued. If anything, his form in December had been his best yet. Chippy was another player who had really seemed to have found his feet. The hurly burly of the Second Division didn't really suit his technical game. He was an incredibly talented footballer, but lacked physicality. There were times, even during the promotion season, when he could be bullied out of a game. In the First Division though, players tended to stay on their feet, it was a lot more reliant on team shape and tactical awareness. Players with a good first touch and good vision prospered. There was even talk of him being on the radar of the England Manager, Howard Taylor.

The Kirkby Karaoke incident, as it had been named, had kick-started Clifton's season. Even with the cold snap that had hit the UK, the players enjoyed coming to training and there was a real sense of togetherness.

Harry, though, was a little wary. He had begun to see signs of fatigue in lots of the players, but he didn't have a big enough squad to rotate. The Christmas period was coming up. The fixtures would be coming thick and fast. Even the big sides had trouble at this time of the year. How was his paper-thin squad going to cope?

Chapter Sixteen

Saturday's game was at home to White City, who were bottom of the league. After the game was the club's Christmas party. Everyone arrived at the stadium with their evening outfits on hangers, ready to change into after the game. The Christmas night out was a notorious date in the footballing calendar. There were always a few professional footballers who would fall foul to it. Nights in the cells or worse. Generally, the drinking started in the changing rooms, especially after a victory. It would then continue until the wee hours. Local night club owners would often offer free drinks to a group of players, knowing that the word would soon get out and their club would be packed out. VIP areas would be set up and the carnage would begin. One year, two young Tottenford players had been sacked following their Christmas night out. A well-known publicist had been paid a substantial amount of money to keep the details out of the papers. Inside of football it was well known that at least five first-team players had also been involved. They were obviously considered too important to fire.

The game itself was a drab affair. White City were lacking in confidence and got as many players behind the ball as possible. Clifton, however, looked off pace. Several players were carrying injuries but had to play as there was no-one to replace them. Ryan and Lee were the two subs. The club covered up the fact that they both were injured and would not be able to play any part in the game. Clifton Rangers even registered Doug and Alex with the Football Association so that they could play if necessary. They were now part of the playing squad in case things got any worse. If White City had known of the issues, they may have been a little more adventurous. In the end, Rangers were pleased to gain a point. It felt like a point won rather than two lost, even with White City's position in the table.

In the changing room, the party started straight away. Harry had bought a crate of beer and it was sitting in the middle of the room.

"I would like to thank everyone, including Doug and Alex, for all your hard work so far this season. We have a week now until our next game. Have a great night, I don't want to know the details. Just look after each other and don't do anything too stupid!"

"Looks like you can't come then Jimmy!" said Reggie, a big smile on his face.

"Shut up you old git and chuck me a beer!"

Harry passed a couple of cans of alcohol-free Kestrel to Ryan and Liam. He then left the changing room to let the players get on with their party.

By the time they got to the players' lounge they were already in high spirits. After a few disapproving looks from some of the bard members as well as a particularly enthusiastic chorus of "Everything I Do", Harry wandered over and suggested it might be time for them to move on to the first bar.

The first stop was at a pub run by a big Clifton Rangers fan. The players would often go there as he gave them discounted drinks and made sure that no-one bothered them. Liam was shocked by how quickly the players were drinking. At about eight, Ryan made his apologies and left. There would have been a time when he would have been nursing a bottle of Jack Daniel's at that point in the evening and in for the duration. He tried not to preach, but he didn't really enjoy being around people who had been drinking anymore. Although he had turned himself around, he knew that his body had been ravaged by his wild days. He had been struggling with the step up this year. Despite the hattrick at Kirkby, it had been a stop-start season for him, niggling injuries had prevented him really managing to get a run of form together.

Liam stayed on, but his mind was elsewhere. He had taken to going the toilet at regular intervals to check for calls from Lisa. even though she knew he was out on his Christmas do and wouldn't be ringing for that reason. By the time they moved onto a club, at about 10.30, he must have been to the toilet about ten times, which attracted funny looks.

The pub had been okay; Liam always enjoyed listening to the older player's stories. They were often shocking. Some of the things players had done in the past were beyond belief. Reggie and Terry had seen some things. They could both tell a story, too. The only time when anyone stopped drinking was when either of them were talking. Everyone was enthralled, hanging on every word. The funny thing was that they were present in every story but never actually spoke about anything they did. Liam was sure that they were the star of most of the stories. Times had changed. Modern players were always in the public eye and had to be more careful. That wasn't to say they had all suddenly become saints. They just had to choose their moments more carefully.

The nightclub was a different matter. Liam hated it from the moment they arrived.

"Alright lads? This way. No need to queue."

One of the two burly bouncers, even Terry was dwarfed by them, led them through the door to a reserved "VIP" area. In truth, it was about three tables and a couple of booths on the second floor overlooking the dance floor. The Venue Nightclub wasn't the sort of nightclub that got many VIPs. First off, Liam didn't like the looks they got from the people who had been queuing to get in to the club. The other players didn't even seem to glance in their direction. Liam could see they weren't impressed with a bunch of flash footballers being allowed to jump the queue. Liam had never actually been to a club. His teenage years had all been centred around his football and he had never really been interested in clubbing. As they entered the club, he couldn't believe how packed it was. It was a good job they had the doorman with them, or it would have taken them ten minutes to get to their seats. The second thing he noticed was that a group of professional footballers was a big deal in a nightclub. He felt extremely uncomfortable.

Liam could feel the hostility radiating from the men as they moved through the club. They clearly saw the team as a threat. They knew that with a group of professional footballers about the pickings would be slim.

Then there were the women.

Liam had no sooner sat down when a blonde girl with a tan that was suspiciously robust for December and an equally suspicious bust, sat next to him. The outfit she was nearly wearing rode up as she sat down. Liam didn't know where to look. She rested her hand on his thigh and gave it a little squeeze. Liam jumped. He wasn't used to this sort of attention.

"Move up, sweetheart, I'm skinny but not that skinny," she said, squeezing in next to him.

Liam looked around, the doorman was clearly only letting women into the VIP area, and they were practically fighting each other to get in. Many were looking in his direction. They knew who he was. He had been all over the news after his impressive start to the season. Liam's star was on the rise and they clearly wanted to jump onboard.

The women who didn't want to get in the VIP area looked at the Clifton team and the girls surrounding them as if they were dirt on their shoes.

The next minute, a couple of hostesses appeared with buckets of ice, filled with bottles of champagne. The blondee girl got up out the booth and grabbed a bottle, popped the cork like an expert and returned with two glasses.

She was not happy when she realised that her ticket to stardom had already gone.

Chapter Seventeen

Liam could tell that something was wrong the minute he answered the phone.

"What's up, Lisa? You sound awful."

"Sorry Liam, I didn't want to bother you. It's this whole uni thing. I can't do it. I'm struggling. I've got two assignments due at the start of January and I haven't even done the required reading yet!"

Liam hadn't heard Lisa like this before, whenever they spoke, she sounded like she was loving university life. He had just presumed that she was smashing it. It broke his heart hearing her so upset.

"Is there anything I can do?" he asked.

"Not really. Not unless you have the keys to a time machine."

Liam was desperate for Lisa to come back for Christmas, but as far as he knew Lisa was following her dream by enrolling at University. He more than anyone knew how important that was.

"Why don't you stay for Christmas? Then you can catch up with everything. Didn't you say Lorna was staying?" Liam couldn't believe he was saying it. He had been looking forward to her coming home since she left. Now here he was, trying to convince her to stay. "We've managed to cope up to now. Besides, we're playing Boxing Day so I'll be in training on Christmas Day. We'd hardly see each other anyway."

On the other end of the line Lisa took a deep breath. She had presumed that Liam wanted to see her as much as she wanted to see him. She had been hoping that he would tell her to come back and quit the course. Not suggest she didn't come back at all.

"If… if that's what you think is for the best. Look I've got to go. I'll... I'll give you a ring tomorrow. Bye Liam," Lisa quickly hung up the phone as the tears started to flow.

Liam stood there, looking at his phone.

What just happened?

Chapter Eighteen

It was turning into a Christmas from hell. The training ground was frozen, so they had to train on the indoor dirt pitch at the ground. It was as cold in there as it was outside. Half the team weren't even training as they all had minor injuries, and the physio had thought that rest was the best remedy. This meant they hadn't been able to work on anything constructive all week and no-one had a clue what the team was going to be on Boxing Day. On Christmas Eve and Christmas Day Doug and Alex joined in with some of the training. It was becoming increasingly likely that one or both might play a part on Boxing Day.

Liam hadn't spoken to Lisa since the ill-fated phone call. That had been three days ago.. He knew it had gone badly but he still didn't get what the problem was. In the back of his mind one thought kept repeating. *Did we break up?*

Going into the Christmas period, Liam was feeling at an all-time low. For him, his release came when he played. In both the game on Boxing Day and the other one three days later he managed to pick up the man of the match award. This was very impressive. Not least because physically and mentally he was on the edge, but also because Clifton lost both games. This meant that Clifton had now dropped back into the relegation places. There was no time to dwell. In four days' time they were up against Mansford City in their first game of 1992.

They had history with Mansford City.

Especially Liam.

This was going to be a huge game; if they were able to get a team out.

Chippy was a no. He had a slight strain on his calf that would not clear up in time. Scott Fulling had pulled his hamstring and would be out for at least six weeks. Reggie was now thirty-three and shouldn't really have played in the last game as he had a trapped nerve in his back. Typical Reggie though, he went out and played anyway. The club was worried that his injury would escalate into something worse and so the coaches had taken the decision out of his hands and declared him unfit for the Mansford game. Harry had let the physio deliver that news. Lastly, Lee McGuckin was suspended, having picked up ten bookings. This meant that out of a squad of sixteen players, there were twelve bodies available for selection.

Harry watched training on New Year's Eve from the tiny room above the dirt pitch. He hated what he was having to do to Liam. He could see in the boy's body language that he was suffering. He looked heavy-legged and was noticeably quiet. Quite how he had managed to keep up the level of his performances was a mystery. A lesser man would have crumbled by now. Harry longed to be able to pull him out for a few games, but his hands were tied. He had to keep Clifton in the First Division. By his calculations, Liam had either scored or assisted on about two-thirds of Clifton's goals. He was undroppable.

Harry had sent his most trusted scout, Len Carlton, off on a watching brief to find some young prospects in the lower leagues. That way, if any money was made available to him then he would be ready. He was confident that Len would find some good prospects, but he wasn't so confident that the Chairman would put his hand in his pocket. He did have an ace up his sleeve, though. There was talk of a huge overhaul coming next year. The money they were talking about was astronomical.

No-one wanted to be relegated the season before the start of the Premier League.

Chapter Nineteen

Mansford City were a huge club with an impressive history. Recent years had not been so impressive for them. They had yo-yoed up and down between the First and Second Division. They had lived in the shadow of Mansford United for a long time. Things were changing. They had wealthy investors from the Middle East and were serious movers in the transfer market. The manager, Trevor Hurlock, was one of the best young managers in football. He had built the team in his mould. Mentally and physically strong and highly competitive. In his time as a player, Hurlock had been   feared. On the pitch, he would use intimidation and menace to get under the skins of his opponents. And he could back it up. He was known to be very handy with his fists as well as his feet. Everyone who had played with him had a story to tell. He didn't suffer fools and had a vicious tongue. His own teammates were often as fearful of him as his opponents. But, underneath it all, he had a good footballing brain and was technically solid. He had been capped eighty times by Ireland. It would have been more, but he had fallen out with several managers who had refused to pick him. City had been promoted the previous year, the same as Clifton, but they had not rested on their laurels. Their investment was paying off, they were currently fourth. Hurlock had recognised that the First Division was not like the Second Division. He had added quality and depth to the squad. They were always ready for a fight, but if a game of football now broke out then they were ready for that too.

And Liam had history with them…

It started in the tunnel.

"No cheap shots today, son. You're going in my pocket and that's where you're staying. I see your bodyguard ain't around no more!" Bryan Smith, Mansford City's captain and enforcer was in Liam's face. Liam could smell the Gatorade on his breath. Smith shoved Liam, sending him staggering back into the wall of the tunnel. Players from both sides jumped in, pushing and

51

shouting, but Smith had made his point. Liam knew he was in for a game that day.

Jason had moved back down the line and was now immediately behind Liam. He would have been no match for Smith, but he was aware that, with no Reggie about, Liam was lacking his normal protector.

"You alright, mate?"

"Yeah, nothing I can't handle, cheers Blackie," replied Liam with more than a touch of false bravado.

"Okay, well stay close anyway," said Jason.

"Come on Wizard, show these kids what real football is!" said a voice from their side.

Liam and Jason looked up to see it was an old steward talking. They followed her eyes to Alex Kempster, who was walking out behind them. He was wearing the number fourteen and was Rangers' second sub for the game. Alex was nearer fifty than forty and had a full head of grey hair.

"Hopefully, I won't need to!" Alex said in response.

Liam and Jason jogged out onto the pitch.

"Wizard?" asked Jason.

"You need to learn your Clifton Rangers history Blackie," said Liam, just before their voices were drowned out by the roar of the crowd greeting the players' entrance to the field.

It soon became clear that this was not the same City from the previous season. They were still dangerous from set pieces as they still had six or seven players who were six foot plus, but they had a bit of quality now too. Sergio Batista, their Argentinian forward, was one of the best forwards in world football, and it was a shock when City managed to sign him. Money had spoken. Andreas Silva, from Spain, was another world-class addition. The first half felt like men against boys. City soon realised, that Liam was the only threat. Ryan looked a yard or two off the pace, he still didn't look fully fit and, without Chippy, Rangers lacked quality. The two replacement players for Chippy and Reggie were not of the same standard. In central midfield, Greg worked hard but the game was too big for him. The City midfield bullied him. He was not long out of youth team football and still developing. He was no Liam. There were few

52

players who could come straight out of youth team football and not lose a step.

Liam was still a threat, but the problem was that, whenever Liam got the ball, he was surrounded by City players. He was also dropping deeper and deeper into his own half to try and get the ball which meant when he did get it, he was a long way away from the City goal. Harry could see that he was getting increasingly frustrated. Harry would have loved to change things but, on the bench, he had Alex, who had not played a competitive game for more than ten years, and the back-up keeper. He couldn't ask for anything more from his players, but they were just not as good as the City team. He looked up behind him to the director's box. The City Chairman had flown in on his own private jet to watch the game, whereas David Salow's seat remained empty. He lived in Clifton but had not attended a game in nearly a year.

"Can't we get ourselves one of them, Clem?" said Harry nodding towards the City Chairman.

"It'd be nice to be able to do the job without our hands tied behind our backs. We were a better team than this lot last year!" said Doug Clemance.

"Not this year," said Harry, more to himself than anyone else.

If it was a boxing match it would have been stopped. Jason and Terry were doing a solid job at the back but going forward it was Liam, and Liam alone, who presented a threat. No sooner did one attack end than another started. Batista opened the scoring on thirty-eight minutes with a good finish past Jimmy Mimms. By half-time they should have been out of sight. It was as if the City players were too comfortable. They were so dominant that they missed chances by trying to be too clever, for example, make one more pass rather than finish the game off. The Clifton players were demoralised at half time. Harry tried to rouse them and pump them up for the second half. They knew though, like him, that they were horribly mismatched. The second half continued much the same as the first. Bryan Smith was now man-marking Liam, following him everywhere. Hurlock had clearly realised that if they could nullify Liam then the game was theirs. Ryan was now noticeably limping, and Harry was forced to send Alex out to warm up.

Liam had noticed that since Smith had started marking him, he was getting a little more space. In the first half there were always three or four players around him, but now they seemed to be leaving Liam for Smith to take care of. After about seventy minutes, Liam received a pass from Greg Hales and managed to spin Smith. He started to break into space with the ball for the first time in the game. Suddenly, his shirt was almost torn from his back as Smith cynically pulled him back, giving away a free kick and stopping Liam's progress. The referee booked Smith, but Smith didn't care. He had stopped the attack and now City players were back in position and organised.

Next came a huge roar from the crowd. Liam and Smith both looked over to the side-line to see Alex taking off his tracksuit top, ready to come on. Ryan limped his way over and shook Alex's hand as the fourty-seven-year-old made his comeback for the club. Alex ran straight over to Liam.

"H says for you to push further forward, I'm going to play up front with you," Alex said.

"Hey Grandad, you forgot your Zimmer frame!" said Smith, laughing.

The other players soon joined in, clearly finding it hilarious that Clifton had to play Alex.

It was obvious from the first time he got the ball that, although he couldn't get around the pitch like he used to, Alex still had ability. For the first time, Liam had someone on the same wavelength as him and they had a couple of nice exchanges of passes. The problem was everything had to be played to feet as Alex could not physically run in behind the City defence. As a result, although it looked good, they never really threatened the City goal. Meanwhile, City seemed to be able to create chances at will. Somehow the score remained 1-0 thanks to some great goalkeeping from Jimmy Mims, some brilliant defending from Jason and Terry and careless finishing from the City players. The game entered the last ten minutes and Hurlock was heard instructing his players to shut up shop. He was clearly happy to take the 1-0 win. Clifton had yet to register a shot on target. As the game entered its final moments, a clearance from Blackie headed in Liam's direction. Once again, he managed to slip past Smith and was about fifty yards from goal with only Alex in support and the whole City defence in front of him. Smith couldn't foul Liam this time as he was on a yellow card. This meant Liam was able to burst forward and drive at the City back four. Three of the City defenders converged on Liam, leaving Alex being marked by the last defender. Without breaking stride, Liam passed the ball to Alex and continued his run. Alex saw the run of Liam and went to return the ball to him. The Mansford defenders did not see Alex as a threat and had stayed with Liam, blocking any attempted pass. But Alex had never intended to pass. Instead, he let the ball run though his legs. His marker had also been more concerned with Liam than Alex and fell for the dummy, trying to anticipate the pass that never came. By the time the Mansford defenders had reacted to Alex, it was too late. Alex was now through on goal at a slight angle. He carefully steadied himself, eyeing the bottom left-hand corner of the goal. Seemingly without looking in Liam's direction, he then reversed the ball back into the path of Liam, who had not stopped running, unlike the Mansford defenders. Liam then ran the ball into the back of the empty goal.

The ground erupted as the whole team, including Liam, ran to Alex to celebrate the goal. Liam may have scored it, but it was a moment of magic from Alex that had created it. When they finally made their way back to their own half, Alex walked past Smith.

"Hey, young man, have you seen my Zimmer frame?" he said, bending over and walking like an old man with a walking stick. The whole stadium erupted, this time in laughter. You could tell that Smith didn't find it quite so funny.

Even in the last couple of minutes, City had chances to win the game. On the touchline, Hurlock was seething. When the final whistle went, the Clifton players practically ran off the pitch. It felt like they had stolen a point and they wanted to get away before someone realised. The crowd gave an extra-loud cheer as Alex made his way off. Jason jogged past Liam, nudging him as he went.

"At least I now know why they call him the Wizard, mate!"

Chapter Twenty

The following week was International Week. This meant no domestic football for ten days while players went off on international duty for their respective countries. For most First Division managers it was a time of worry. Particularly for the bigger teams who would have most of their squad off travelling around the world. Managers of these sides would be hoping their players would be returning injury free and not suffering from fatigue. For Clifton, it was a godsend. They had no internationals in the squad. Harry was hopeful that by the time of the next game they would have a fully fit squad. That day's game had left a bad taste in his mouth. He felt his first-choice side was a match for most teams in the league. Unfortunately, he knew the squad was lacking in depth, and today had been the proof in the pudding.

At the end of the match, Harry had checked on the health of all the players. Those with knocks were expected to report to the physio team at the training ground on Sunday. Everyone else was given the week off to recuperate. By the time they got to the players' lounge, some of the players were already planning trips away.

Liam took the news of a week off badly. Football had been a welcome distraction to him, the last thing he wanted was time to dwell on his relationship with Lisa. He knew that he needed a rest, but he had always been someone who would play every day if he could. A week with no football, alone with just his thoughts for company sounded like hell.

In the lounge, Harry sidled up to Liam.

"You okay?" he asked.

"Yeah Boss," Liam lied.

"Well, you might want to tell your face; you look like you've found a penny but lost a pound. I meant what I said about everyone resting. You more than anyone. Your body's still growing, you need to let it repair. I don't want to hear about you running around the pitch or working out in the ballcourt. I've already told Johnny to chuck you out if he sees you. He seemed more than happy with the idea."

Liam just nodded his response. He knew Harry was right, but it didn't mean he liked it.

The conversation, if you could call it that, with Liam had clearly bothered Harry. He expected Liam to be tired, but Liam had looked miserable. It didn't make sense. Here he was, a huge Clifton Rangers fan. Playing week in week out for his boyhood club. Not only that, but he was playing out of his skin. Harry knew that Ted Braxton, England's chief scout, was in the crowd watching that day's game. Liam should have been buzzing.

Harry made a mental note to visit Liam's flat at some point in the week and see if Liam's mum could shed any light on what was bothering him. He knew from experience that she made a good cup of tea.

Chapter Twenty-one

Liam's mum decided to act on Tuesday. She had barely managed to get a word out of him since Saturday's game. She knew what the problem was, and Liam moping around the flat for a week was not going to solve it.

"Liam, babe, can I come in?" she said as she knocked on his door.

Liam was still under the covers, even though it was nearly midday. If anything, that just showed his mum that she had done the right thing.

"Here you go," she said, chucking him an envelope.

"What's this?" he asked as he satup.

"Train tickets. I've got you on the 1.20pm so you need to get up and jump in the shower. You've got no chance if you turn up at Lisa's looking like that."

"But mum,"

"No buts, Liam. You need to sort this out, face to face. Get up there and tell her how you feel. You can't carry on like this."

Liam was about to argue, but knew there was no point. He had even thought about doing it himself but had needed the push his mum was giving him.

"I've phoned the university and there's a Travelodge nearby. I've got their number for you. I'll pack a bag for you while you're in the shower."

***

The closer he got to his destination, the worse the idea seemed to get. The train was just pulling into South Netfield Station. Liam had had a lot of time to think about what he was doing on the four-and-a-half-hour train journey. It really didn't seem like a good idea anymore. It didn't help his nerves when he was recognised at the train station and had to stop and pose for several photos. Netfield was home to two huge football clubs which had fallen into decline. Liam wasn't sure how welcome he would be, so he didn't hang around for long.

It was a ten-minute walk from the station to the university. Liam had to fight the urge to turn around and return home. He had rehearsed over and over in his head what he was going to say during the journey. In the end he need not have bothered.

In his head, he had pictured himself knocking on the door of her room and then telling her of his feelings for her. What happened was that pretty much the first person he saw on entering the campus grounds was Lisa. She was walking with her head down towards Liam, who was standing in front of a campus map trying to find her dorm. Lisa walked past him at first, but something made her turn back.

"Liam?"

"L – L - Lisa..." Liam stuttered, suddenly unable to string a sentence together, his carefully rehearsed speech instantly forgotten.

In the end, they didn't need words. The minute they saw each other they both knew. All their doubts and insecurities melted away.

It had been more than six months since they had last seen each other. Six months since their first kiss. That kiss, like this one, had said much more than words ever could. It was like a weight had been lifted from both.

"Wow, Osborne, you're a sight for sore eyes," Lisa said, a smile lighting up her face. She was slightly shorter than Liam, with dark straight hair hidden below a blue New York Yankees cap. She was dressed for comfort in a grey tracksuit and battered old Converse trainers. To Liam she looked perfect. She was *his* Lisa.

"Have you grown? I don't remember having to stand on tip toes to kiss you!" she said.

"So everyone keeps telling me."

It was like they had never been apart.

Being a huge Clifton fan, Lisa wanted to know everything about the season so far. Although they had spoken on the phone, it had been different. Here, now, in person, the two of them barely took breath. They spoke all the way across campus to her room and long into the afternoon, sitting on her bed.

Eventually Liam began to get hungry.

"Let's go across to the uni bar, we can grab some chips," said Lisa.

"I don't know Lisa; you don't know what it's like these days. It's a nightmare, we won't have any peace."

"Behave Mr Osborne, you're not that famous. This can be like our first date," Lisa always called him Mr Osborne when she was teasing him. It was what he had called himself when they first met; it had been his first day at the club, and she was the receptionist that showed him around.

Liam soon gave in. She had that effect on him. It was to prove a costly surrender.

Chapter Twenty-two

It was Liam's phone that woke them up.

The night before had gone just as Liam had predicted. Word had quickly got around that he was in the bar and it had soon become packed. Everyone had wanted an autograph, a picture or just some of his time. Lisa could see why he had been getting annoyed with it. They had only been there about half an hour when she could take no more. The worse part about it for her were the girls. She understood the boys. They were all football fans, and quite respectful of her. But the girls were just rude. It was like she wasn't there. They were flirting and hanging all over Liam. She counted herself fortunate that he was oblivious to it. It made her even more conscious of the extent of her feelings for Liam. In the end, they bought some crisps and beat a hasty retreat, not even waiting for their chips to arrive.

When they had got back to the room, they had carried on talking deep into the night. Lisa told Liam that she was thinking of quitting her course. She was relieved to see a smile appear on Liam's face when she told him. It was a relief, after the telephone call about Christmas she had really thought he didn't want her to come home. In the end, they had fallen asleep almost in mid conversation.

***

Liam answered the call still half-asleep. His vision was blurry, but he could see that it was still 8.00 in the morning.

"Hello," said Liam.

"Liam, it's Harry. You need to get yourself back to Clifton right away. I've got a car on the way. Don't speak to anyone until you've seen me. Especially not the press."

"What's going on Boss?"

"It's all hit the fan Liam. I don't want to say too much on the phone. But the Chairman is kicking off, we need to get it sorted."

At that, Harry hung up the phone.

Lisa looked across at Liam. She could tell by the tone of his voice that something was wrong.

"What's up?" she asked.

Before Liam could answer, there was a knock on the door. Lisa opened it to see Lorna standing there. She had a concerned look on her face. In her hand she held a copy of The Globe. There, in the bottom right corner of the back-page was a picture of a young couple kissing. Even if she hadn't recognised the blue Yankees cap in the picture, Lisa could clearly see one of them was her. The blonde mop of hair gave away the other person.

The headline simply said: FAMILY AFFAIR.

Chapter Twenty-three

The car arrived at about midday and turned out to be Johnny and his minibus. Despite Liam's protests, Lisa insisted on travelling back with him. Liam was dreading getting back to Clifton. When he first joined the club, he had been told by Jason that a youth team player had been released for getting too friendly with Lisa. Then, last season, Billy Butler had been released just because the Chairman had suspected that he had been going out with Lisa. He had been wrong. What would happen to Liam? He was thankful that Lisa had decided to travel with him as just having her near to him gave him strength. He was going to need every ounce to get through this. It also meant he didn't have to spend the whole journey with just Johnny as company.

Harry was there to meet them at Clifton Park and explained that they were going straight to the Chairman's office.

"He hasn't said anything about you Lisa, so you might want to stay down here in reception," Harry said.

"No, Mr Welch. If Liam doesn't mind, I'm going with him. My Dad needs to know that Liam and I are a united front."

"Well, okay, if you're sure."

"I am."

Liam held Lisa by the hand and the three of them made their way up in the elevator to her father's office.

Mr Salow's secretary told them all to go straight in.

As soon as they walked in, they saw The Globe newspaper on Mr Salow's desk. It had been screwed up. Not a good sign. The Chairman was standing behind his desk. He was dressed immaculately in a designer suit and black tie. His grey hair was slicked back, and his face was red. Another bad sign. He wasted no time.

"What the hell do you two think you're up to? How long have you been going behind my back?"

"Sorry sir, we didn't mean to. I mean, it wasn't intentional. Going behind your back I mean. Yesterday was the first time we'd seen each other since Lisa left for Netfield," said Liam.

"So how do you explain this, then?" said the Chairman, throwing the paper in Liam's direction.

Liam didn't know what to say and there followed an awkward silence. In the end, Lisa broke it.

"That's none of your business, Daddy. I can see who I like, and so can Liam. I'm not a child anymore."

"It becomes my business when it affects the good name of this club. I have a good mind to sack him."

"Hold it there sir. Liam is our best player. Without him we wouldn't have a chance in hell of staying up," said Harry. "And you know the talk. If the Premier League happens, and we aren't in it, then it could cost us millions."

Lisa stepped up to the desk, so she was directly opposite her father.

"The good name of the club! It's not exactly a secret how you feel about this club. If Grandad could see what you were doing to his Clifton Rangers." She paused to compose herself. "Anyway, you can't sack him, he's done nothing wrong. I don't work for the club anymore, which means he hasn't broken any club rules. You can't do with him what you did to Billy."

"Fine, maybe I won't sack him. If I can't sack him, I'll sell him," said the Chairman.

"Please, Mister Chairman. I beg of you. Liam is the heart and soul of this side. We can't replace him," implored Harry who could see the whole season going up in smoke.

"Don't worry Boss, I'm going nowhere," Liam said. "Clifton Rangers is in my heart. I have nearly four years left on my contract and you can't force me to leave. I'm sorry that you found out about me and Lisa the way you did, sir, but this isn't just some childish fling. Lisa and I love each other, so you're just going to have to get used to it."

"Please, Daddy, if you really cared for me then you'll support us with this. Because Liam's right, we're going to be together whether you like it or not. But it would mean the world to me if it was with your blessing. I know you want what's best for me. Please, trust me Daddy, Liam's what's best for me. Please don't make me choose."

Mr Salow was visibly shaken by Lisa's words; it was obvious she meant every word. Everyone knew him for the ruthless businessman he was, but Lisa was his only child. With her mother's passing, Lisa was the only family he had. He turned away from them a moment, clearly lost in thought. After a few seconds he turned to face them again.

"This has all been a bit much for me. Look, Lisa, you're all the family I have, and all I want to do is protect you. I'm not happy about this, but I'll respect your feelings and there'll be no repercussions. But, young man," he turned the Liam, "if you ever slip up, if you ever hurt my baby girl, then I don't care what you mean to this club or how much money it costs me; I'll make it my business to destroy you. That is a promise."

Harry decided this was a good time to make a quick exit. He started to shuffle Liam and Lisa out the room. Lisa paused briefly and turned back to her father.

"Thank you, Daddy," she said before turning and leaving the room.

"Right you two, I'm off. I was supposed to be having a few days away with Ange, and she isn't happy. See you next Monday, Liam. Please stay out of trouble!" said Harry.

"Will do, sorry Boss," said Liam.

Harry went off ahead. Liam and Lisa followed on behind, still holding hands.

"Do you realise you actually told my Dad you love me before you told me?" said Lisa, finally allowing herself a smile.

"Oh God, I did didn't I? I did mean it, but that wasn't the way I wanted to tell you. Why do we always do things the difficult way?" said Liam, who then appeared to remember something. "Did he really say he was going to destroy me?"

"I think he did Mr Osborne, so you'd best be good to me."

"I can't believe the most important person at Clifton Rangers hates me."

"Hate's a strong word. Let's just say I don't think you'll be invited over for Sunday dinner anytime soon."

Chapter Twenty-four

Wednesday's game was an FA Cup tie against Thamesmead Town. Thamesmead were a non-league team who played in the Conference League. They had won nine games to get to this point in the competition, having started back in August. It was now the third round proper, where the teams from the top two divisions joined the competition. Liam knew that the players were pleased with the draw and were already thinking about the next round. The only negative was the fact that they were drawn away from home. Sometimes the lower-league teams switched grounds so they could get a bigger pay day by playing in front of a bigger crowd. Clifton had asked Thamesmead, but Thamesmead had refused. Clifton were going to be travelling to South East London for the game.

It was Tuesday morning, Liam, Greg and Jason were playing piggy out front with the youth team. This had become a regular occurrence and it was good for the youth team players to try and match the first team players. Sometimes, other players like Chippy and Scott Fulling joined in. But as the mornings had grown colder, the more experienced players had sought refuge in the heat of the changing rooms, often only emerging when they heard Doug's voice calling them out.

It had been just over a week since the meeting with the Chairman and everything seemed to have calmed down. Lisa had returned to Netfield to get everything straight. She had decided to come home, this at least had cheered her Dad up a bit as he hadn't wanted her to leave to study in the first place. Liam was now just looking forward to getting back to playing again.

"Liam, get up here." Doug's booming voice came from the upstairs window of the house at the training ground.

"Yeah, em sure," replied Liam.

"Someone's in trouble."

"Who's been a bad boy?"

"Did you forget to do your homework?" came the calls from the other players. Liam laughed he knew that professional sportsmen and women are basically kids who never grow old.

They are like the Peter Pans of society. They have gone from playing games with their mates in the playground to playing games with their mates as a job. Being called in to see the Boss is like being called in to see the headmaster. Everyone assumes you're in trouble.

Liam walked inside and up the stairs, wondering what he had done wrong.

He knocked on the door and was told to come in. Liam hated getting called in by the manager. Even if you hadn't done anything wrong, it was a chance for the coaching staff to analyse your performances in training or matches. Generally, they were not kind. You just had to stand there while they bounced of each other. Criticising your effort, your form, your fitness, your weak foot, your heading and even your appearance. Nothing was considered sacred. Liam was the best player at the club, but he still dreaded what was to come.

"Sit down," said Harry.

"Have you got a mirror, Liam?" said Doug.

"Why?" said Liam.

"Because you could do with a haircut," said Doug. "You look like you just got out of bed you scruffy git."

Here we go, thought Liam.

"Spot on Clem, but, anyway, that's not why we called you in. I just received a call. You've won the First Division Player of the Month Award. Congratulations," said Harry.

Liam felt himself going red. He nodded his thanks.

"They're going to present it before the game on Saturday," said Harry.

"Wow, I don't know what to say," said Liam.

"You don't need to say anything, just don't get too big a head," Doug replied.

Liam took his cue to leave and was relieved to be getting off lightly. First Division Player of the Month? Him? He hadn't seen that coming. He caught his reflection in the glass of the door as he left the house. Perhaps a trip to the barber might be a good idea. As he re-joined the game of piggy, the first few snowflakes began to fall.

Chapter Twenty-five

The orange ball rolled, there was a thin layer of snow that attached itself, but it definitely rolled.

"Game on!" announced the referee. He picked up the ball and carried it inside with him. The orange ball was only brought out for snow-covered pitches and he wasn't about to lose it.

The two managers returned to the changing rooms to pass on the 'good' news. The Thamesmead manager looked more pleased than Harry.

When Clifton had first arrived a the ground, they had been sure that it was going to be postponed. It had been snowing since Friday morning and, overnight, it had been like a blizzard. The conversation on the coach had even turned to what the team was going to do with their day if the match was postponed. Thamesmead had called for help from the local community on the radio and they had managed to get all the lines uncovered. Everywhere else sat beneath a blanket of white. The ground itself was a million miles away from what Clifton were used to. In some parts of the ground, the only thing that stood between the fans and the players was a piece of rope hung between two poles. You couldn't really call it a stadium. It had stands on all four sides, but there were large gaps between them where there was nothing at all. In the gaps were piles of snow that the supporters had cleared. It gave the ground an odd, disjointed look.

"Right lads, get yourselves changed the game's on," said Harry, trying to sound enthusiastic. The players all groaned.

The changing rooms were tiny and freezing. They had a small heater high on the wall, but the light bulb was probably giving off more heat. Alex was doing strappings and rub downs in the shower area and even that was a tight squeeze. The players had one peg each and there was barely enough room to hang their clothes. There was a lot of swearing going on as players cursed the cold, the lack of space and how run down everything was. The floor hadn't even been swept. It was so bad that a few of the players speculated that Thamesmead had done it on purpose to upset them.

Meanwhile, in the Thamesmead changing room, the players were pumped and desperate to get started. For them, it was the biggest game of their lives. They would have played on nails if they had to. For them, the facilities were what they were used to. They couldn't wait to get started.

Temperatures were rising even as the snow fell...

Doug was fuming. It was only the warmup, but he could see that the players' minds weren't right.

"For Christ's sake lads, wake up. Get your hands out your sleeves and sharpen up. You've got a game to play!"

His words were lost in the sleet that was now falling. Not one Clifton player had consciously decided to take their foot off the gas. But it was as if everything had taken them down that road. The snow, their recent good form, the low level of their opponents, the ramshackle ground. Everything was telling them that this was a game to just get past. Win it and go home. But that, of course, is not how life works. The Clifton players had allowed their intensity to drop, it wasn't easy to switch it back on again.

It started to go wrong seventeen seconds after kick off. Liam passed the fluorescent ball to Ryan, who passed it back to Chippy. Chippy took a touch and looked at where to pass it. He spotted Scott Fulling in space on the wing and took another touch to set himself up for the pass. The ball didn't quite roll as he expected due to the snow, so he had another touch. That proved to be a mistake. The Thamesmead forward, a huge man with tree trunks for legs, launched himself into the tackle, putting everything he had into the challenge. In the First Division, it would have been called a foul, perhaps even a booking. But they weren't in Kansas anymore. The referee waved play on while Chippy lay on the floor, clutching his calf. The ball ran free and was now halfway between the Thamesmead forward, who had just got back to his feet, and Scott Fulling. There was only going to be one winner. Scott dangled a foot, but it was a huge mismatch and the Thamesmead player comfortably came away with the ball. The conditions meant he couldn't really run with the ball so instead he just kicked it into the space behind the Clifton defence and chased after it. He was quickly followed by his fellow forward, who might even have been slightly bigger than him. Clifton somehow smuggled the ball out of play, but the pattern of the game had been set. It wasn't really a football match. You couldn't pass the ball very well and you certainly couldn't dribble. It came down to who was up for it the most. It was no contest. It was only a lack of quality that stopped Thamesmead from being in front. They won every challenge and harried and harassed Rangers' players at every opportunity. Chippy looked like his calf was troubling him, which meant Clifton were virtually a player down in the centre of the pitch. Ryan also looked to have picked up a knock and had been a passenger for the majority of the first half. Add to this the fact that as it got colder the snow began to turn to ice, which meant it was turning into an ankle breaker of a pitch so some of the Clifton players were wary of getting injured. Terry and Reggie were the only two players who seemed to be up to the challenge. They seemed to be enjoying themselves.

Harry rarely lost his temper, but at half time he went ballistic.

"It's just a battle. It's not a game of football. If it was, you'd win. If you don't match them physically, you'll be out. Greg and Lee, go get warmed up, you're going on. Ryan and Chippy, you're coming off, we need fit bodies out there and you're both struggling."

Harry looked around the room.

"Boys, you can't play out there. Win it and move it. Get the ball in their half. Chase down *everything*. Liam, it's going to just be you up front. Get hold of it and try and win some set pieces. Remember, these are part-time players. They won't have your fitness. They'll tire. Change of shape too. We're going three at the back, Lee's going to go alongside Terry. Jason you cover them both. Lads, I know it's tough out there. We'd all rather be playing on a carpet at Tottenford, but we aren't. As Churchill once said, if you're going through hell, keep going!"

Harry's half-time talk seemed to help. The second half was more of an even battle. Greg brought hard work and effort to the midfield, while Lee McGuckin as the extra centre half seemed to give the team a little more stability. It was an awful game of football. It began to resemble a World War I battle. Grown men fighting over a few feet of ground. Both Jimmy Mimms and the

Thamesmead keeper had been largely unneeded and were in more danger of frostbite than conceding a goal.

Harry had been right, though. The Thamesmead team were starting to show signs of slowing down. The Clifton Rangers players trained every day and were obviously at the peak of their fitness. The Thamesmead players all had full-time jobs and trained a couple of evenings a week. There was no way Thamesmead could have kept going at the pace they were. About midway through the half, a mistake by the Thamesmead central defender, yet another beast of a man, let Liam in with his first opportunity for a shot at goal. He was on it in a flash. The central defender slid in to try and make up for his mistake, leaving Liam in a heap on the floor. The defender protested his innocence, but the referee had already blown for the foul. The free kick was right on the edge of the area and was one step from being a penalty.

Liam knew this was their best chance so far. He carefully stepped out his run up. He had decided to hit it hard and low, hoping that the icy surface might make it difficult for the keeper. He took a deep breath and started his run up. Just as he was about to strike the ball, he slipped on a particularly icy patch and lost his footing. He made a comical sight as his legs went from underneath him. The ball sliced off his foot, spinning harmlessly through to the goalkeeper. Or at least it should have. Either the spin of the ball or the snow meant that the ball never quite made it through. Scott Fulling had been running in for any rebounds. It was now a clear race between the keeper and Scott Fulling to get to the ball. Scott was a tricky winger but not renowned for his bravery. The keeper came sliding out feet first, expecting a challenge, but Scott was already jumping out the way. The ball caught him on the back of his leg and rebounded back past the keeper over the dug-out goal line and into the snow in the back of the net. It was the luckiest goal you were ever likely to see. Scott ran off celebrating to the fans behind the goal as if he had just scored the goal of the season. He soon realised it was the Thamesmead fans at that end when he was hit with a barrage of snowballs. He quickly retreated, much to the amusement of the rest of the team.

The match continued as it had before. It was full of effort and endeavour but not one for the football purists. For all their

71

efforts, Thamesmead never really troubled the Clifton goal. In the end, Jimmy Mimms said it was the easiest game he had ever played, with not one shot on target.

"It was certainly the luckiest game, first Liam slips then it just hit Scottie for the goal," said Reggie.

"Twice," added Liam.

"What do you mean twice?"

"I actually slipped twice, once getting the free kick, then taking it."

"You mean..."

"Exactly, he never touched me. I slipped on the same bit of ice both times. Should never have been a free kick in the first place."

Chapter Twenty-six

The game against Thamesmead seemed to be just the wake-up call that the club needed. It focused the players, showing them they couldn't afford to take their foot of the gas. Harry saw a renewed energy in training that they carried into their matches. Harry had also been able to select his strongest starting eleven. The next three league games brought five points, which meant that they went into their fourth-round FA Cup fixture unbeaten in the new year.

The draw had again been favourable to Clifton. They were drawn at home to Petersmouth from the Second Division. The priority for the season was always staying in the First Division. The two favourable draws had not gone unnoticed by the fans or players. The FA Cup had always held a special place in the heart of Clifton Rangers. It was the first major trophy of the Jameson years and they had won it on no fewer than seven occasions during the club's heyday in the seventies. No-one was speaking about it, but it was certainly on everyone's mind.

The game itself was very straightforward. There was to be no repeat of the complacency from the Thamesmead game. In front of a watching Howard Taylor, the England manager, two goals from Liam and a free kick from Chippy gave Clifton a comfortable three-nil victory.

***

"Liam, babe, can you pop to the offy and get me a pack of cigs," came the call from the kitchen.

"Mum, I'm on the phone, besides the draw's in a minute," said Liam. He had always hated getting cigarettes for his mum from the off licence. Even as a kid she used to give him a note and send him off. In the end, he didn't even need the note. Mr Poles, the owner of the off licence, would just see him and say, "Twenty Lambert and Butler?"

"Sorry Lisa, it's just mum again. Here we go, they're just starting," said Liam, turning the TV up.

Liam and Lisa had been in touch pretty much every day since it had all blown up. Lisa had quit her course and was going to be

73

returning to Clifton at the end of the month. Liam had been trying to convince his mum to let her stay with them. His mum had said no. That was why she had decided to see out her four weeks' notice in Netfield then come home to her Dad's. Maybe by then he would have calmed down a little. Or if not, an answer would magically appear.

Right now, they were on the phone with each other waiting for the live draw for the fifth round of the FA Cup. They didn't have long to wait as the first ball out was number seven Clifton Rangers – another home draw. Ball number twenty-four was second, which meant Clifton were once again kept away from the big guns of the First Division with a home game against Buxton Rovers.

"Buxton Rovers," came Lisa's voice on the other end of the line, "that's a great draw. They're having a nightmare season. They've only won two games all season, none away from home."

"We thought Thamesmead was going to be easy," said Liam.

"We won't make that mistake again. We win the next game we're in the quarter finals."

It was funny, one of the reasons he loved Lisa as much as he did was her love of football. It meant that she understood him, it also meant that he had someone to talk to. Someone who understood. It could be embarrassing sometimes, though, as he knew that she knew more about football than he did. He didn't know how Buxton were doing this season, yet he knew she could probably name their whole team.

"Lisa," said Liam.

"Yes?"

"Do you think that if we are ever out with other people you could pretend that I, the professional footballer and First Division superstar, actually knows more about football than his girlfriend?"

"First Division superstar?! You've changed, Mr Osborne. But, yes. I guess I can dumb myself down a bit for you. God knows, there's no way you can up your game to my level!"

From the kitchen, Liam's mum could hear Liam laughing. It made her smile. Since his return from Netfield he had been a lot more content. She had tried to get the full story from Liam. But again, like most teenage boys, he wasn't the most eloquent. What she did know was that this wouldn't have happened if he was still working at her brother's garage.

"Okay, no worries I'll speak to you tomorrow. I should be home by about two."

Liam's mum could hear the conversation winding down, so she made her way back into the living room. She found it all far too awkward being in the same room as Liam when he was talking to Lisa. If she ever walked in on a conversation, his face would immediately turn red and he would start mumbling into the phone. At first, she had quite enjoyed doing it, accidentally on purpose, but it had soon grown old.

Liam's mum arrived in the living room, Liam quickly said his goodbyes and put down the phone.

"Finally, don't know what you two talk about, you only spoke to her yesterday."

"okay, well I'm finished now."

"That's good, you can go get me twenty Lambert and Butler now."

Chapter Twenty-seven

Between the Petersmouth game on the 27th [of] January and the Buxton tie on the 15th [of] February there were another two League games to navigate. A penalty from Ryan gave Clifton a one-nil victory against Solent in the first game. The penalty had been won by Liam after a surging run. In the second game, they managed to grind out a nil-nil draw against Balham Palace despite not being at their best. This result pleased Harry the most. He knew that in a long season you were not always going to play at your best. Picking up points when you didn't play well was a skill. Against Mansford City when they drew, they hadn't deserved it and were lucky, whereas against Balham they were resilient and hard to beat. He knew that with Liam on the team, if they could stay in games, they always had a chance. Even against Balham he had created some good opportunities. The Balham game also stretched their unbeaten start to the 1992 season to seven games. They had now opened a four-point gap between themselves and the relegation places. They were no longer favourites for relegation and some pundits even had them down for a mid-table finish.

Liam felt like he was on top of the world.

Not just because of Clifton's and his good form.

Lisa was back.

Lisa had been living in her Dad's mansion on the top of Clifton Hill and they had been spending every spare moment together. It was crowded at Liam's mum's flat, but there was no way Liam was going to hang out at the chairman's mansion, especially after the last meeting. Liam's mum thought the world of Lisa, but the situationin the flat were getting tense.

"You do realise it can't go on like this for much longer, don't you?" said Lisa.

"What can't?" said an oblivious Liam.

"Seriously? Your mum was looking at holiday brochures last night. I've been round here every night for the last two weeks. My dad has started referring to the house as Hotel Salow," said Lisa. "You know you're going to have to come over to the house at some point. We'd hardly see Dad anyway, he's always in his office."

"Okay, okay. Look, we've got the big game on Saturday, I'll get that out the way then how about I come round for that Sunday dinner you spoke about?"

Chapter twenty-eight

The "Big Game" was right.

Clifton had gone FA Cup crazy. Everywhere you went all you could hear was talk of how this was Clifton's year. The lucky win over Thamesmead, the fact they had been drawn at home against lower-league opposition. Twice. The fact they were unbeaten in 1992. Everything was in their favour. Now that their league form was consistent, and it looked like they were going to stay up, everyone's minds had become focused on the cup. Even though it was only the fifth round, Clifton Park was sold out. The only sellout of the day. Even the sun had made a winter appearance.

Since she had returned, Lisa had not seen a game. She hadn't even visited Clifton Park. With the article in The Globe, she had been worried that she would be recognised. Her father was still hugely unpopular with the Clifton crowd and she was scared some of that resentment would be transferred to her. Especially as her Dad never went to any matches anymore. The other reason was Liam's form. He had been playing so well this season that she was concerned that if she went and he played badly that it would somehow be her fault. She had been around footballers her whole life, and she knew this was how they thought. As silly as it sounded, there was still a bit of her that didn't want to risk it. She was still a Clifton Rangers fan at heart.

"Are you sure you don't want to come? It's nonsense, you know that right? As if you being there will make any difference to the result."

"I know, I know. But still, I would never forgive myself if you lost," said Lisa. The sound of a horn could be heard from outside. "Here's Blackie now, good luck. Not that you need it."

Liam kissed her goodbye and made for the door.

"You still coming mum," he shouted back over his shoulder towards the kitchen.

"Of course, Babe," came the none-too-enthusiastic reply from his mum.

Lisa and Liam both laughed.

Even though he knew it was nonsense, as Liam made his way down the stairs, he was relieved that Lisa wasn't going to be at the game. There was no point in upsetting the footballing gods just before such a big match.

***

Lisa was a nervous wreck. She had been listening to the game on the radio in her room at her Dad's house. It had been all Clifton, but the Buxton keeper was having one of those days. The commentators were almost laughing as they announced another fine save. Lisa had taken to pacing up and down, unable to sit still. In her mind, she was kicking every ball. There was now just over ten minutes to go.

"By my reckoning, that is the eleventh save by Greg Smith in the Buxton goal. Another fine effort by Liam Osborne, but it is increasingly not looking like his, or Clifton's day," said the commentator, Mark Hanson. In his day, Mark Hanson had been an incredibly successful footballer.

"I agree, Mark, and we all know that Buxton's sloping pitch will be a huge advantage to them if it goes to a replay. Clifton have got seven players out there who have appeared in every game this season. Fatigue is sure to play a part. And with the replay scheduled for Tuesday night, you sense that Clifton really need to get the victory today to keep their run alive," said Brian Motson, the other commentator.

Lisa swore at the radio, but she knew they were right.

The game continued, with Clifton unable to beat Greg Smith, who appeared unable to do any wrong. Clifton were getting more and more desperate, throwing players forward at every opportunity.

Lisa couldn't stand it, she had to do something.

Meanwhile back on the radio.

"I make it nearly time now Brian," said Mark Hanson.

"I agree, I think we must just be moving into any injury time the referee wants to add," replied Brian Motson. "And here's a rare Buxton attack. Mark Grigg has the ball on the left wing and swings in a good cross, but Terry Johns wins the header easily. He and Blackmore have been faultless at the heart of the Clifton defence today. Bradley Carpenter picks up the ball, but he has no options, the Clifton players look exhausted."

"Not all of them Brian, have a look at young Liam Osborne. He seems to have managed to get some energy from somewhere that's a great run forward if Carpenter has seen him…"

"And he has, that's a great pass; it was as if he already knew that Osborne was going to make that run before he made it."

The sound of the crowd could be heard rising behind the commentators' voices.

"But here comes Smith charging out of his goal, this is now a race to the ball between him and Osborne. I think Smith has a slight lead," continued Motson.

"Hold on Brian, Osborne seems to have gone through the gears he's going to get there first."

"And he has, he knocks it past the keeper, he must sc- no wait Smith has caught him. He's down, that must be a free kick," said Motson.

"And a sending off Brian. Osborne had an open goal if it wasn't for Smith."

"You could be right, but wait, the referee's waving play on. He's seen McCoughlan following up. He was the only one alive to the situation, he must score. He's got an empty net ahead of him. Goal!!! And McCoughlan scores. That must be the winner. Clifton Rangers are surely through to the quarter finals with that Ryan Mccoughlan goal!" Brian Motson was having to shout now to be heard above the cacophony of sound coming from the Clifton crowd.

"McCoughlan may get the goal but the credit must go once more to Liam Osborne, what a discovery this kid is. the sky's the limit for this kid, mark my words Brian!" said Hanson.

Out on the pitch, the whole Clifton team raced to Ryan to celebrate in front of the crowd in the North stand, behind the goal. As he ran, something made Liam turn around. He looked up at the West Stand. He just had a feeling…

Lisa was going crazy just like everyone else at the stadium. She was still slightly out of breath following her mad run from the Mansion on the hill to her seat in the West stand. At least she now knew she wasn't a jinx.

Back in the commentary box, Brian Motson was asking the question.

"So, Mark, the big question. Can Clifton go all the way? You have been here all day, the same as me. You've heard the Clifton fans saying it's their year, that their name's on the cup. What do you think?"

There was a pause as Mark Hanson contemplated the question.

"I don't think so Brian. They're a young side, you don't win anything with kids."

Chapter Twenty-nine

No sooner had the elation of victory subsided than Liam remembered his deal with Lisa. He tried to worm his way out of it. He had tried everything. He was tired from the game. He had a stomach ache. He didn't like roast dinners. In the end, he had put his foot down and told her that he was an adult, and he could make his own decisions. He was not going and that was that.

Liam pressed the buzzer.

"Hello? Hi. It's me, Liam," he said into the intercom. The gates swung open and he made his way up the gravel drive. The day before, he had played in front of 35,000 people and not had even the slightest nerves. Yet here he was with butterflies in his stomach, feeling like he was going to throw up.

The front door opened, and the smiling face of Lisa greeted him. She looked amazing.

"Why hello, Mr Osborne," she laughed as she saw the look on his face. "Don't worry, it's just dinner. No-one's died."

"Not yet," he mumbled under his breath.

The house was incredible. Liam thought you could probably have a five-a-side game in the hallway. It reminded him of a library or a church with its high ceilings and leaded windows. The dining room was off the hallway through a vast doorway. The table was already set, and David Salow was seated at the head of it. He barely looked up from the newspaper he was reading. The dinner was an experience that Liam would never forget. It was a traditional Sunday roast, but not the carvery that you might get at a carvery like The Royal Oak. The food was all brought out in serving bowls. Yes, brought out. Lisa's dad had servants. Liam didn't know where to look. He wanted to serve himself, but thought it rude to do so. Instead, he just nodded when offered food, and tried not to look too embarrassed. It was the best roast Liam had ever eaten. Probably the best meal he had ever had. Liam's mum wasn't much of a cook. She didn't really have the time. Most of his meals were either straight out the microwave or the chippy. The closest he had been to a chef had been standing next to the school cook. Lisa tried to make him feel comfortable, talking about the previous game. Her dad, on the other hand, barely spoke and looked to positively bristle every time football was mentioned. It was one of the most enjoyable, most awkward meals ever. Dessert was a home-made apple pie with custard. Liam couldn't get enough, but after his third slice Lisa suggested they go off to her room to listen to music.

"Good that your stomach ache seems to have cleared up though," she said.

Despite the pull of another slice of apple pie, Liam was glad to be given an escape route. The look on David Salow's face showed he wasn't the only one relieved the ordeal was over.

As soon as they got to Lisa's room, Liam started. This was too good an opportunity to miss.

"You've got servants! How posh are you?" said Liam.

"We do *not* have servants! Mrs Greaves is more like a friend of the family. It has been tough for Dad since Mum died."

"So, you don't pay her?"

"Well, yes, of course we do but,"

"And does your Dad do the cleaning?"

"No, we have a cleaner…"

"And that's a big garden you've got…"

"Okay, I get the point."

"Then there's the Bentley. I'm pretty sure it's not your dad who drives that…"

Lisa decided this was not an argument she was going to win, choosing instead to give Liam a "friendly" jab in the arm.

"Oy, careful your ladyship. Haven't you got a butler who does your fighting for you? You might break a fingernail."

"Shut up, Mr Osborne," she said smiling. "Don't forget you also work for my Dad. So, does that make you his servant too? Maybe I'll get Dad to get you to do a few jobs around here."

Liam decided to quit while he was ahead.

Chapter Thirty

Dinner at the Salows' did make life for Lisa and Liam a lot easier. Liam's flat was too crowded for them to really have any privacy. But at Lisa's house, they pretty much had the run of the place. It was so big that they rarely even saw Lisa's Dad. Liam was sure he did his best to avoid them. Not that he minded. The Chairman was still an intimidating figure, and Liam was very aware of the power he held over him.

Other than the spectre of David Salow, the three-weeks building- up to the quarter final were some of the happiest Liam had ever known. Lisa had watched every game and, although Clifton did finally suffer their first loss, they won the other two games, which meant they were on fourty-eight points. Noone had ever been relegated with fifty points, so they were now just two points away from guaranteed safety. In truth, fourty-eight points would probably be enough and relegation was no longer being talked about. They were starting to look upwards. A top-ten finish was a possibility. Ted Braxton, the England scout, had also been to all three Clifton games since the cup win. The football rumour mill was suggesting that Chippy would get a call up for the Senior squad and that Liam was a shoe in for the U21s. There had also been other good news. Stuart Richards, Lisa's old Boss at Clifton's press office, had been in touch and offered Lisa a job. Officially, it would be the local paper that she worked for, but her job was the junior on the sport's desk, with the local team as part of her beat. This meant that she got to spend a lot of time at the club. It also meant that, as Lisa was not officially working for the club, then Liam wasn't breaking any rules. Things between the two of them were starting to get serious. Now that they had two incomes, they had become regular visitors to the estate agent in the high street. It seemed to be a case of when and not if they would move in together.

Their focus though was the quarter finals, and March 8th soon arrived.

Once more the draw had been kind with another home game. They had been kept away from the big guns and, although they were playing a First Division team for the first time, it was Chorley who were languishing in the bottom three.

"Okay lads," Harry said. "I don't need to tell you what a big game this is. Don't play the occasion, play the game. If you stick to what you've been doing this year, then there's only one winner. Don't panic, don't get too excited, don't try to do anything more than you do every week. Play your normal game. It's a mistake to try to look too far ahead. The chain of destiny can only be grasped one link at a time. This is our next link."

There were a few knowing looks around the room. Harry Welch loved a Churchill quote, and the players were always on the lookout for his next one.

It was another full house at the match and nerves were to prove decisive. Within five minutes, the Chorley centre-half misjudged a clearance and only succeeded in slicing the ball into his own goal. The early advantage settled any Clifton nerves, while it compounded Chorley's. Clifton barely needed to get out of third gear. Ryan and Liam grabbed a goal apiece, and the final score was three-nil, but in truth it was a lot more comfortable than that. The outcome was never in doubt from the moment the first goal went in, perhaps even from the moment Harry gave his team talk. The only negative was Ryan having to be withdrawn on the hour mark, this time with a tight calf. He cut a very frustrated figure as he made his way up the tunnel.

The radio went on the minute the players returned to the changing room. The last of the quarter finals were all taking place at the same time as Clifton's game. Following the other games played that day, in the hat for the semi-final were Clifton, Mansford United, Tottenford and the surprise package, Leyton. Leyton were closest team to Rangers geographically and were currently sitting second in the Second Division table. The draw was to be screened live on Monday night. No-one said it, but Leyton was the team that everyone wanted to be drawn against in the semi-final.

Chapter Thirty-one

"Mansford United! I bloody knew it!" said Liam.

Liam and Lisa were in her room watching the draw on the BBC. As if they needed to be told, the presenter on the TV gave a bit more context.

"So Mansford United, the reigning league champions and current league leaders, are drawn against newly promoted Clifton Rangers. Mansford, who are on course for an incredible quadruple, will go into the game as overwhelming favourites. The whole country will be rubbing their hands together in anticipation of a Tottenford, Mansford United final."

Lisa turned the TV off.

"At least you get to play at Wembley," began Lisa. "Makes Wednesday's game interesting."

Clifton had yet to play Mansford United, the first meeting had been cancelled due to Mansford playing in the European Cup and it had been re-arranged for Wednesday. It would have been a no-lose game for Clifton. If they were beaten, everyone would have expected it. If they managed to get a point or win, then it would be a bonus. Now, suddenly, it had taken on greater significance. It would be a chance for one of the teams to put down a marker before the semi-final. As usual, Clifton were hopelessly outmanned. Mansford United had the deepest squad in the league. Their reserve side would challenge for the title. They were in the League Cup Final, the week before the semi- final. They were also one game away from the European Cup Final. They topped their group with a game still to play. A draw in the final game in the European Cup would be enough for them to book their place in the final, also at Wembley. In the league, they were four points clear of Tottenford with a game in hand. Although they had played more games than anyone else in all the European leagues, they seemed to be coping due to their large squad. Clifton, on the other hand, were not in such good shape. Ryan had been ruled out for three weeks with a calf strain. Greg was also out with shin splints, a sure sign that he had been overused. They were having to manage his game time to try and nurse him through to the end of the season. But, at some point, he was going to have to be rested, possibly for as long as six months. Reggie was still having issues with his back. Terry Johns, who was in his thirties, was not training during the week, instead he was on the exercise bike every day, only coming out the day before matches to work on set pieces. Liam and Blackie were still ever present, but were in desperate need of a break. There wasn't a player who didn't seem to be nursing some sort of ailment.

Harry sat alone in his office on Tuesday morning, contemplating the whole situation. In normal circumstances, he would just see out the season and try and add to the squad in the summer. If anything, the FA Cup had been less of a blessing and more of a curse. He was seriously worried about the damage he was doing to Liam and Blackie. He knew he had used them far too often during the season. The situation with Greg Hales brought it home to him. Greg had played less games than either Blackie or Liam, but he had a stress injury that could have been avoided. He was brought out of his thoughts by the sound of Doug calling everyone out for training. They were just going to have a light warmup followed by a few set pieces that might come up in the next game He had at least three players who would just be watching the session due to injury. All three would be involved in the game itself. Two of them would be starting. Whatever the score, he knew that he would need to have a difficult conversation with the Chairman soon. It was true that he did have a long-term plan, but that would not be coming to fruition any time soon. Right now, he had to come up with a more immediate plan to get Clifton through to the end of the season without inflicting too much damage. Plus, there was the small matter of the FA Cup semi-final to win.

Chapter Thirty-two

Liam sat on the Clifton Park turf. He was struggling to breathe, and his lungs felt fit to burst. Other than in the South Stand, an eerie silence filled the ground. He looked up at the scoreboard to check that it had really happened.

0-7.

He didn't know it, but it was the biggest home defeat in Clifton history, comfortably beating the previous 0-4. They could have no arguments. As Lisa would say to him later, Clifton were lucky to get zero. Liam, like every Clifton player, had spent ninety minutes chasing and harrying with no real effect. Mansford seemed to score at will. It could and should have been ten. The crowd didn't know how to react. They had stayed with Clifton all through the game. They could see that the players were giving everything. But everything wasn't enough. By the end of the game, they had been down to ten players. Harry was forced to take off Blackie after seventy minutes. He had gone down with cramp and was barely able to walk. Harry had already brought Reggie off after sixty minutes. Mansford had sent scouts to watch Clifton on many occasions. They were known to be meticulous in their preparation. Reggie had been struggling with his back for weeks, and they had clearly targeted him. Ryan Wilson gave him the run around from the moment the game kicked off. It seemed like every pass went in his direction. It was the first time in his career that Reggie had been glad to see his number held aloft. Then, with ten minutes to go, Scott Fulling had gone down with an ankle injury. No-one saw how the injury happened.

At the end of the game, Harry didn't know what to say. He felt proud of the effort his team had given him. No-one's head had dropped. They had given him everything they had. It hadn't been enough. The truth was the squad was neither big enough nor good enough. That was the Chairman's fault. Not the players. It was time for action.

Reggie sat slumped on the bench. He did not change or shower until long after the other players had left. He just sat staring at the wall, lost in his thoughts. A few players tried to offer words of encouragement, but he either did not hear or just didn't acknowledge them. Even Jimmy Mimms didn't offer a joke about his performance. They could see he was hurting. He resembled a lion that had lost its place at the head of the pride.

Thursday morning, the players were told that they were not training, but that they still needed to report to the training ground.

The mood was sombre as the players made their way into the changing room. Harry, Doug and Alex were already there. All three of them had stayed at Clifton Park into the early hours, working out details for the next four-and-a-half weeks.

Harry told them all to take a seat and began to talk, "Right boys, I can only imagine how you're feeling. I want to start by saying I'm proud of every one of you. You can hold your heads high. What you've achieved this season has been nothing short of miraculous. What I'm going to say is going to sound like we've given up. But it's the opposite. For us, this season is now all about the game on the 17th of April. We're safe, the league games are no longer our priority. We have five games between now and the semi-final. Many of you will only be playing a small part."

Harry went on to explain that, with immediate effect, he was putting in a programme aimed at getting everyone at their physical best by 17th April. Some players would not be playing at all to try and clear up the injuries they had been carrying for months. Other players would be having periods of rest where they also would not be selected. The youth team would be taking up the slack, filling in where needed.

"But Boss, we'll get hammered. You're talking about six or seven first-team regulars who are barely going to put on a shirt," said Terry.

A lot of the other players nodded their agreement.

"We're also going to be without Alex and Doug for most the matches, as they're going to be watching Mansford's games. That's why we're having this meeting. We all need to agree on this. We must understand that it's going to be tough. None of us like losing. The crowd aren't going to like it. But I'll be giving a press conference and I'm going to tell everyone exactly what we're doing. We may get punished by the F.A. I'm even prepared to pay the fines myself if I have to. Then, if the fans choose to still come to our games, they know what they're letting themselves in for. We only have two home games out of the five, anyway. But for this to work, we must stick together. We also need to be thick-skinned. It's no use doing this and then turning up for the semi-final with our confidence shot to pieces. We need to delete these games from our minds."

The conversation went back and forth but, in the end, everyone agreed. Reggie, Scott and Terry were sent off to the physio room. Every other player who was carrying an injury was told to report there as well. Everyone would be given a plan by the physio to ensure that they would be one hundred per cent fit by the time they next played. The club had paid for a back specialist to come in and treat Reggie over the next few weeks. The rest of the squad were sent home to rest. There was to be no training on Friday, but all the available players were told to go for a light jog Friday afternoon in preparation for Saturday's game. Jason and Liam were told that they were to go home and rest. They were to report back to training on the 8^{th of} April. At various stages over the next four-and-a-half weeks every player in the squad got at least a week's break from football.

As expected, the results suffered. On the first Saturday they were beaten 5-0. A reasonable result considering no less than seven youth team players were in the starting eleven. By the time the F.A got round to fining the club for fielding an understrength team, they had lost two more games, 6-0 and 5-1. Harry paid the majority of the fines, but the other players all agreed, led by Reggie, to contribute a percentage of their wages. The fourth game was much closer. Several of the players, including Terry, were now back from their physio programmes and cleared to play. With just three youth team players in the squad, they only lost 3-1. The final game before the semi-final was a good contest. Liam and Jason were back, and both played an hour. Ryan completed his second ninety minutes since his calf injury and Reggie played the whole ninety minutes and reported no issues with his back. Following the Mansford United game, Reggie had worked tirelessly at his rehabilitation. A couple of the other injured players swore that he was carrying around a picture of Ryan Wilson with him. One of them was sure they heard him growl at it on one occasion. They drew the final game 1-1, with Ryan scoring the goal. When Harry looked around the changing room, he liked what he saw. The players still appeared in good spirits and, other than Greg Hales, everyone was fully fit. They now had a week of training to put into place the plan for Mansford United, based on Doug and Alex's reports.

On Sunday, Mansford United won the League Cup against Mansford City. They then had their final European Cup group game on the Wednesday, which they also won, booking their place in the final in May. The quadruple was still very much on.

Chapter Thirty-three

While Mansford had been winning the League Cup, the Clifton players had been called into the ground. A TV had been set up in the changing room and all the players received a booklet when they entered the room. Harry, Doug and Alex proceeded to fully explain the plan for Saturday's game. In the booklets the players were given was a detailed report on Mansford United. More specifically, a report on the players they were up against. It included a list of strengths and weaknesses. Things like which foot they favoured, and what they normally did in specific areas of the pitch, including ways of taking advantage of this. Harry then explained the overall game plan. It was given the name Rope a Dope, and this was written on the front of all the booklets. Some of the players got the reference, and when Harry put on the video it all became clear. The players were instantly on board. There was only one part of the plan that was changed.

"I don't need that," snarled Reggie when offered the booklet.

"But Reggie," began Alex.

"*I don't need* that," He repeated. "Is it my job to take care of Wilson?"

"Well, yes, but…"

"That's all I need to know."

The look on Reggie's face told Alex that there was no point in pursuing the matter further. He looked across to Harry, who gave a shrug. Harry knew Reggie well. He wondered if Ryan Wilson realised the hornet's nest he had disturbed. He felt sorry for him. For a second.

***

Training that week went well.. It was purely focused on the game plan. Every player knew their job and was clear on what to do. There had been a serious edge to the week. The normal banter had subsided. Everyone was completely focused on the job in hand.

Harry had decided that, breaking against the Wembley tradition of staying over night in a hotel, they were going to travel down by coach as usual. Mansford, meanwhile, were staying in the allocated hotel; they had been there so often in recent times that they were on first-name terms with the staff. Harry did not want anything to distract his team from what they had to do. The approach to the stadium was something else. Every player stood and moved to the left of the bus as they drove towards the stadium along Wembley Way. The first thing they saw were the iconic twin concrete towers, that had dominated the London skyline for more than seventy-five years, keeping watch over the famous stadium like the Queen's guards at Buckingham Palace. Not a word was spoken. Every young boy or girl dreaming of being a professional footballer in England had two dreams; to play for England and to play at Wembley. Wembley, the spiritual home of the beautiful game. The FA Cup was the most revered competition in the world and there was a time when it ranked alongside any competition in the world, including the European Cup. To everyone on the coach this was a dream come true. If they had needed it, this was a moment to bring them even closer, united in their resolve.

The warmup was unique in the fact that one player did it by himself. Reggie warmed up on the halfway line. He didn't once take his eyes off Ryan Wilson. You could see that it was unnerving Wilson. On several occasions, Wilson miss-controlled the ball. At one point a ball hit him on the head while he was glancing in Reg's direction. It brought some laughter from the building crowd. Reggie did not laugh.

The ticket allocation for Clifton had been 35,000, with Wembley holding 90,000 fans in total. The tickets had gone on sale two weeks before the final and had sold out in three hours. Mansford United had 45,000 season ticket holders and so the stadium was a sell-out. Amazingly though, there were gaps in the corporate section of the stadium where they received free tickets. A crime considering the number of real fans who could not get a ticket.

Clifton won the toss and kicked towards the East Stand, where the Mansford fans were situated. This was part of the plan and the first victory of the day. The game kicked off to a wall of sound. As in the first game, the ball was transferred quickly in Ryan Wilson's direction. Wilson took the ball in his stride ready to run at Reggie. As the ball had been passed to Wilson, Reggie had already started running. Wilson did not even see him coming. Reggie's timing was perfect, he made contact with the ball at the same time as Wilson did. Scientists could have broken down what happened into some sort of clever equation involving momentum, force and impact. All anyone in the stadium knew was that it looked painful. Very painful. The ball, and Wilson, landed on the dirt track that ran around the pitch. Wilson very nearly landed on the greyhound track that lay beyond that. The roar of the Clifton crowd rivalled that for England's famous victory twenty-five years before. That moment set the tone for the Clifton display. Lee McCullogh came into the defence as a third centre half in a back five. The two wide players, who normally played as attackers on the wing, sat just in front of the right and left back. Liam was withdrawn, playing almost in midfield. Ryan was on the bench. He did not seem to mind; he knew his part in the day was still to come. When Mansford got the ball, they were faced with two banks of five players. There was no space to play. The Clifton players seemed to know their every move. The first forty-five minutes passed with neither team managing a single attempt on goal. For the neutral supporter it was an awful game. Clifton had parked the proverbial bus, leaving a packed defence between the opposition and the goal. No matter how hard they tried Mansford had no way around it. They still tried to stick to their game plan of getting the ball out to Ryan Wilson. But he had become extremely hard to find. Partly because he had Reggie almost attached to him, like a snarling dog on a lead, and secondly because he didn't seem too keen on having the ball. When it did come his way, he also seemed very eager to move it on to someone else. He resembled someone playing a game of Russian Roulette, unsure when the bullet was going to arrive.

At half time, Harry, Doug and Alex called for more of the same.

And so it continued.

Mansford were getting increasingly frustrated. They had started to go more direct, playing longer passes, but that played into Clifton's hands even more. They were also beginning to look tired. Wembley was a particularly unforgiving pitch. Players were known to go down with cramp and exhaustion. Even with

Mansford's big squad, they had played an incredible number of games. Harry could see the signs of fatigue appearing in Mansford's play and careless mistakes as they became physically and mentally fatigued. Clifton, on the other hand, had conserved their energy by sitting back and letting the game come to them. They were looking fresh and rested.

Rope a Dope had been a tactic famously used by Muhammad Ali. He used it in his fight against the much stronger world champion George Foreman, in their infamous Rumble in the Jungle. In the early rounds, Ali pretended to be trapped against the ropes, goading his opponent into throwing ineffective punches. When he felt Foreman's punches losing their snap due to fatigue, Ali changed tactic and went on the attack. The exhausted Foreman was unable to defend himself and relinquished the world title to Ali. Harry knew that it was time for the second part of their plan. Mansford had started to lose their snap, time to go on the offensive.

At seventy-eight minutes, Ryan came on for Lee McCullogh. He had played his part in the plan to the very letter. He shook Ryan warmly by the hand.

"Over to you," he said.

Mansford did not know what hit them. The two wide players were pushed back up field. Ryan went up front and Liam joined him. Suddenly, Mansford were on the back foot, they had no answers. Clifton were attacking towards their own fans. Chippy was dictating the game from the middle of the park. Ryan looked sharp and fit; his movement was causing problems for the Mansford back four. Liam was unplayable. The wide spaces of the Wembley pitch gave him space to play. With the shackles removed, every Clifton attack passed through him. And there were a lot of attacks. First, a stinging shot from Ryan following a great Liam through pass brought a good save from the Mansford keeper. From the resultant corner, Blackie won a far-post header that was then scrambled over the line by Ryan. One-nil to Clifton. There were two more good opportunities for Clifton, only prevented by a mixture of good luck and desperate defending from the Mansford players. Then, in the eighty-fourth minute, a long ball over the top by Chippy was latched onto by Liam. He was clean through on goal. The Mansford keeper raced from his line, but there wasn't a person in the stadium or watching at home who doubted that Liam was going to score. He proved them right, side stepping the onrushing keeper before dispatching the ball into the goal. The whole team, including Jimmy Mimms, raced to celebrate with him in front of the Clifton faithful. The goal had been the one that he and Chippy had plotted in preseason training. It was also the same trick that had put Liam in on goal in the quarter final. Mansford's preparation had not been as meticulous as they had thought.

The second goal effectively finished the game. Mansford were spent. The only question was whether Clifton might get a third but, in the end, it finished 2-0. At the final whistle, the shell-shocked Mansford team made their way from the pitch. Ryan Wilson was the first down the tunnel, even though he was the furthest away. They left the Clifton players on the pitch celebrating with their jubilant fans; a famous victory that no one had expected.

Then came the news.

In a day of shocks, Leyton had beaten Tottenford. Dean Beadle had been sent off in the first half for dissent. Tottenford had held on for nearly an hour with ten men before conceding a late goal.

Suddenly, Clifton had become favourites for the FA Cup.

Chapter Thirty-four

Harry felt that, with the euphoria of victory in the air, it was as good a time as any to tackle the elephant in the room. The whole season had been a constant uphill battle due to their sparce squad. He genuinely felt that with some additions, they could have been challengers. This meant one thing: an exceedingly difficult conversation with the Chairman.

"Come in."

This was a conversation Harry had rehearsed many times.

"Thank you for seeing me at such short notice, Mr Chairman."

"Yes, yes, get to the point," said the Chairman, not even looking up from a pile of papers that he was signing.

"Yes of course, sorry Mr Chairman. It was just last time we spoke, back in January, the topic of the Premier League came up."

"I remember the conversation well."

"Err, yes, well. Anyway, I was reading that the Premier League is going to be worth a lot of money for the club."

The chairman nodded still not looking up.

Harry quickly continued.

"And, as you know, we have been working with a ridiculously small squad. We really need another four or five players. Otherwise, I can't see us staying in the division next year. The report I read suggests that the money will increase every year, so it would cost us a great deal if we were relegated. I wondered if maybe I could use the TV money or prize money to invest in some more players. It *would* be an investment."

Finally, the Chairman looked up.

"I do understand, I've been giving it some thought. At the shareholders' meeting they had concerns over the squad size too."

Harry also knew this. He always got the minutes of the shareholders' meetings.

"I tell you what I propose. I'm not willing to fund any signings out of our day-to-day profits and certainly not out of my own pocket. I recognise that you've done a passable job by keeping us in the division this year. The FA Cup is a financial bonus I didn't expect. Maybe it is time to see what you can achieve if I loosen the purse strings a little. Therefore, you can have the TV money that we receive for next season. I will leave it entirely up to you how you use it."

"Can I have that in writing Mr Chairman?"

"Of course, tell my secretary on the way out to prepare it for my signature and to forward a copy to the shareholders."

With that, the Chairman dismissed Harry with a wave of his arm. Harry was happy to leave, before the Chairman changed his mind.

As the door closed the Chairman finally stopped looking at his paperwork.

Mr Welch, you poor fool, thought the Chairman. *If you have survived and prospered in business as long as I have, you learn a few tricks. Number one, always make sure you have all the information. I know Greg Dyke, the person leading the Premier League movement. He is also Chairman of ITV. My sources tell me that they will pay no more than £20 million a year for the privilege of screening the Premier League. That means we will have no more than £500,000. In one fell swoop I have pacified the shareholders and you. There's a reason I live in a mansion, drive a Bentley and am considered a giant of business. You may be good at what you do, but I am the best at what I do.*

Outside, Harry was in the lift. He kept it quiet, but he was a good businessman himself. He had quite the portfolio and many friends in important places. One of his friends worked on Fleet Street. If what he had told Harry is true, then the Chairman may well have signed up for more than he bargained for.

Chapter Thirty-five

There was still the matter of five more league games to complete before the cup final. Harry tried to rotate the squad as much as he could, again using a few of the youth team players. Ultimately, he was happy with the two wins and three losses that came their way. Clifton's final position was a respectable tenth place. They finished fourteen places above the relegation zone, by all accounts a great achievement.

The most important thing was that, going into the final preparations for the big day, Clifton were relatively injury free.

In some ways, the preparation for the Leyton game was more difficult than for the Mansford United game. Then, Mansford had been clear favourites, so a lot of the game plan was centred around stopping them. The final would be different. Leyton may well have won promotion from the Second Division, but they were the underdogs for the final. This meant that Clifton were the team that were going to be expected to go out and win the game. Harry was sure that Leyton would try to do to them what they had done to Mansford. Much of the training had been based around breaking down a packed defence. But as Mansford had found out, this was one of the hardest things to do in football. This time Clifton did stay in the hotel overnight.

"Right lad's it's one o'clock. Start making your way onto the coach," shouted Doug in his usual dulcet tones.

Immediately outside the hotel were about three hundred Clifton fans waiting for a view of their idols. The players all made their way out to the waiting coach. They looked immaculate in their cup-final suits and club ties, even Liam's hair looked relatively tamed. For the players, this was another one of those moments that they would have dreamed of as a child. Cup Final Day in England had always been huge, with the whole day effectively given over to TV coverage on both ITV and BBC. In a young football fan's life, it was only beaten by birthdays and Christmas. In the TV studios, the presenters would have been cutting live to the hotel to catch the teams setting off on their journey to the stadium, complete with a police escort.

The TV crews then joined the players on the coach. They briefly spoke with Harry, before moving on to talk to some of the players. The first person they headed for was Liam. The TV crew practically raced down the coach to get to him first. He was fast becoming one of the most spoken about players in English football. They were sorely disappointed when they were met with a shy, red-faced twenty-year-old who could barely string a sentence together. When they got to Jason, they were even less impressed as the interview was drowned out by a chorus of "Everything I Do".

Before long, the team could once again see the twin towers, and faces were pressed against the glass. Already there were crowds everywhere. The club allocation for the final was less than the semi-final. In the final every club in England received an allocation. In the end, there were just 50,000 tickets to be shared equally between Leyton and Clifton.

The coach drove through a huge entrance in the side of the stadium which dropped them almost at the changing room door.

Johnny sent the players out onto the pitch while the changing room was set up for the game.

When the players came back, everything was in place, and the team was up on the board. They had all known the side for a week due to the work they had done in training, but everyone still nervously checked it. On paper it was probably their best side. The players looked nervous, and Harry's team talk was all about playing their natural game, and not to get caught up in the day. The nervousness sat like a ball in the room. There was little talking, every player seemed to be caught up in their own thoughts. For Liam, the pre-match rituals seemed to drift by as if in a dream. His mind felt like it was caught in a fog. When he looked around, he could see what he was feeling reflected in the faces of the other players. It all seemed so unreal. Almost like they were at home watching with everyone else. Getting changed, warming up, one last pep talk, back out on the pitch, meeting Princess Diana, singing Abide with Me and then lining up ready for kick off. It was like someone else was controlling their bodies, walking them through the day.

The whistle blew.

Leyton had won the toss and spun the teams round. Clifton were going to start the game by kicking off towards their own fans. The referee's whistle seemed to snap the players out of their daze, like a hypnotist clicking his fingers. The players were now animated, shouting encouragement at each other, eager to start. The crowd roared as Clifton took their place in the other half. Ryan stood with his foot on the ball, waiting for the whistle to blow again for the start of the game.

Then they were off.

It was a nervous, cautious game. Both teams knew that one mistake could decide it and no player wanted to be the one to make the mistake. The shape of the game had become clear very quickly. Leyton were happy to get everyone back behind the ball and force Clifton to make all the running. Leyton were very well organised and had clearly worked hard on what they were going to do. Whenever Clifton got the ball, they immediately dropped deep, almost challenging Clifton to break them down. All season Leyton had played with two forwards, but for that day's game they had sacrificed one of them to have an extra defender. That extra defender's job was to follow Liam around the pitch and never give him a moment's space. Clifton had found it exceedingly difficult to get the ball to Liam and, as a result, had been largely toothless. After forty-five minutes, it was still a stalemate. Leyton went in the happier of the two sides.

There was not a lot that Harry could do. They had expected Leyton to defend like they had, but it didn't make it easier to break them down. He didn't have any options on the bench that would make a difference.

"Look, well done lads. It's not easy playing against a packed defence. Keep passing the ball, try and drag them out of position. In the end they'll make a mistake, we just have to make sure we make the most of it. Whatever happens, don't get complacent. Remember us against Mansford? If they score, then we're in trouble. Keep your discipline, don't do anything daft trying to chase the game. Liam, don't make it easy for your marker. He's obviously been told to follow you everywhere, but I don't think he has your fitness or speed. Start running him around. Take him away from where you want to go then try and lose him with changes of pace and direction. Don't let him stand still for a second. I don't think he's the brightest, I actually thought he was going to be sitting down next to you at half time."

The second half continued in much the same way. Liam took Harry's advice and dragged his marker into areas that he didn't want to be in. He started running to the wing then sprinting back into the middle of the pitch and demanding the ball. It seemed to be working. On several occasions, he received the ball in front of his marker and was able to start to influence the attacks. From one of those moments, he managed to find Ryan in the Leyton box and it was only a good save from the Leyton keeper that stopped the opening goal.

After about eighty minutes the game was still 0-0, but you could tell that the Leyton players were tiring as they started to make little mistakes. Gaps were beginning to appear, and Clifton were starting to look dangerous. Once again, Liam had dragged his player out wide and was running back towards his own goal almost in the right-back position. He could tell from his marker's heavy breathing that he was struggling. The ball was at Chippy's feet about twenty yards outside the Leyton penalty area. Chippy had lots of time because the Leyton players had all dropped off, the same as they had all through the game. In front of him was a wall of bodies. Suddenly, Liam changed direction and started to sprint back towards the Leyton goal. His marker was left trailing behind him. Chippy saw Liam out of the corner of his eye coming up behind him. Chippy played the ball perfectly into Liam's path. All the Clifton players were marked, but it didn't matter.

Liam was not passing.

Not this time.

Liam glided past the Leyton midfield who were just too late to respond. He was now onto the Leyton defence who were so deep they were already in their own area. As Liam slowed his approach, his marker had started to make ground. Liam could sense him coming up on his left shoulder and cut across his path, meaning his marker had to check his run to avoid running into the back of Liam. The last defender now knew that he had to make the challenge. Liam, though, was ready and slipped the ball through the defender's legs and accelerated again into the space. He was now clean through on goal, with the keeper advancing. But his marker had carried on running and, just as Liam was about to shoot, he caught up. He was Leyton's last chance and threw himself into the tackle. The challenge was clumsy and that of a tired player. Liam tumbled underneath it, sandwiched between defender and keeper. Just audible above the noise of the crowd was the referee's whistle signalling a penalty kick. Liam's marker received a yellow card. He was fortunate it wasn't red.

Ryan was on penalty duty; a silence came over the crowd as he placed the ball on the spot. He paced out his run-up then paused, waiting for the whistle. When it came, he strode forward confidently and struck the ball cleanly towards the bottom right corner. The goalkeeper had taken a step in the wrong direction and was helpless. Several Clifton players were already moving forward to congratulate Ryan. Unfortunately for Ryan and Clifton, the ball struck the base of the post before spinning, almost apologetically, into the arms of the keeper. Ryan fell to his knees in anguish. If he could have commanded the earth to open up and swallow him whole, then he would have done so. Several other Clifton Players fell to the floor in despair.

Leyton, on the other hand, burst into action. The goalkeeper, looking like a man who had just won the pools, held the ball for a couple of seconds, almost in shock, then the roar of the Leyton fans snapped him back to the moment. The goalkeeper recognised what had caused the crowd's reaction. Clifton only had one player back in defence. The others had all been completely focused on the penalty. The lapse in concentration Harry had warned about. One of the Leyton players had been at the sideline by the halfway line taking a drink, unable to watch what was happening. Now he was off. The keeper launched the ball in his direction. It was now a race between the Leyton player and Terry Johns, the last Clifton defender. Fortunately for Clifton, Terry got there first, sticking out a long leg to divert the ball to safety. The Leyton player, though, was only a second slower and instead of safety the ball only found his chest and ricocheted into the vast open spaces of the Wembley field. The Leyton player now had an empty half to run into. Jimmy Mimms was Clifton's last hope. For a moment, it looked like the Leyton player had taken a heavy touch, tempting Jimmy to charge off his line. But from the depths of his energy stores, the Leyton player found enough in his legs to get there first and poke the ball past the floundering Clifton keeper. Both players lay on the Wembley turf looking back towards the goal as the ball trickled forward, barely having enough power to cross the line. But it did. The Leyton player had gone from zero to hero in the space of eighty-seven crazy seconds.

Liam's shadow for most of the game had scored the goal that was to give lowly Leyton their first major trophy. The cameras were to later show that the Leyton player, the same player who had given away the penalty, was in tears. His manager could be seen consoling him on the touchline. Those tears of pain had turned to tears of joy less than a minute and a half later.

The name of Paul Westwood was to go down in FA Cup folklore.

At the final whistle, Harry and his coaching team were straight out onto the pitch. Harry made a point of shaking the hand of every one of his players. Lifting tired bodies up off the turf.

Once again, he knew that his players had given him everything. Sometimes in football, though, it just isn't your day.

"Come on boys, up you get. Stand straight and proud. Listen to that crowd. They're as proud of you as I am."

He was right. Despite the unfortunate loss, the Clifton crowd could still be heard above the Leyton fans.

"We'll support you ever more,
We'll support you ever more.
Clifton Rangers, Clifton Rangers.
We'll support you ever more,
We'll support you ever more.
Clifton Rangers, Clifton Rangers," rang out around the famous old ground.

The players made their way down the pitch one more time to clap their devoted supporters. There was not a dry eye amongst them.

Back in the changing room, there were more tears. A distraught Ryan dropped his runners-up medal in the bin. Doug quietly fished it out. He knew that once the memory wasn't so raw, Ryan would want it. No-one said anything meaningful. Some of the older pros went around patting the other players on the back and shaking hands. To a man, they all consoled Ryan.

There were no repercussions. They were united in defeat as they were in victory.

Harry only spoke briefly.

"Don't forget this feeling. Hold onto it like a new-born baby. Remember it. Use it. Winning feels like everything. But it's our losses that shape us, build our character, improve us. Success isn't final, failure's not fatal, it's the courage to continue that counts. One day, you'll be able to call on this memory, and on that day, you'll banish it for ever. Now get yourselves changed. The first round's on me!"

He didn't realise how prophetic those words would prove to be.

Chapter Thirty-six

Two days later, on May 11th, the breakaway league signed a broadcasting rights contract with Sky and the BBC valued at £304 million over five years, the largest such agreement in the history of British sport. The Premier League was born. Despite leading the creation, Greg Dyke was ultimately outbid. It was to cost ITV greatly. It was to cost David Salow even more. Each club was to be given £13.8 million over the subsequent five years.

By Harry's calculation, that was a little over £2.7 million a year. Harry wondered if the Chairman might give him the whole five years' worth in one go.

On hearing the news, Harry was straight on the phone to Len Carlton.

Chapter Thirty-seven

Lisa had been brilliant for Liam in the days immediately following the final. Liam's mum didn't really get what the big deal was, whereas Lisa felt Liam's pain.

On the same day as the new Premier League was officially announced, there was an announcement that was to greatly improve his mood.

England had a pivotal friendly with Brazil on May the 17th. Howard Taylor had selected a squad of twenty-eight and put four players on standby for this game. He was then going to cut that squad down to his final squad of twenty for the European Championships in Sweden that summer. Although not in the twenty-eight, Liam was thrilled to be one of the four standby players. He was even more pleased when he saw that Jason Blackmore was also one of the four. In a huge boost to the club, Bradley "Chippy" Carpenter was in the twenty-eight players. Chippy had represented England several times in his early twenties. It was a credit to him that he had turned his career back around. Liam heard the news from his Uncle Gary, who had seen it on Ceefax. Liam being Liam, he had missed the calls from the secretary at the FA to inform him that he was on standby.

Right up to a couple of hours before the game, Liam was checking his phone. It felt strange hoping for someone else's misfortune. But he did anyway. A turned ankle, a bit of flu, an ingrowing toenail. Anything! But it wasn't to be. The game was a 1-1 draw. Chippy was an unused substitute.

Two hours after the end of the game, Liam's phone rang.

Both he and Lisa jumped.

"Hello," said Liam.

"Hello, is this Liam Osborne?" came the voice on the other end of the phone.

"It is."

"Okay, can you hold, I am putting you through to the England manager, Howard Taylor."

Liam's phone trembled in his hand while he waited.

"Hello, Liam?"

"Hello sir," stammered Liam.

"No need for sir, young man. I'm the England manager not your headmaster. Look, I wanted to speak to you personally. You're someone we've been watching very closely. To be quite honest, if you hadn't already played so much football this year, you'd have been in the last two squads. I've very high hopes for you, but I feel like I need to protect you. For this reason, I'm afraid you've not made the final twenty."

Liam took the news in his stride. He had never really thought he would be in the twenty anyway, although Taylor's words made him think that he may have been closer than he thought.

Taylor continued, "I also feel like I owe this current squad a chance as it's them that have got us to the finals in the first place. Be sure to rest up this summer, Liam. Look after your body. It's the tool of your trade, treat it right. You're very much in my plans going forward."

"I will do sir, I mean Boss, I mean Mr Taylor," Liam could hear Howard Taylor laughing on the other end of the line. "Just one thing; did Blackie or Chippy make it?"

"If by Blackie and Chippy you mean Mr Carpenter and Mr Blackmore, then I can tell you that Mr Blackmore didn't make it. Like yourself, he needs a bit more time. But I'm pleased to say that Mr Carpenter has indeed made the final twenty. Tom Holton, unfortunately, damaged his quad in tonight's game. Mr Carpenter has taken his place."

"Get in Chippy!" shouted Liam down the phone, forgetting himself for a moment.

"And on that note, I'll bid you farewell. Hopefully see you soon, and don't dwell too long on the final. I'm sure you'll have many more in your future," said Howard Taylor, chuckling as he spoke.

"Oh yes, sorry, bye sir, I mean," Liam realised he was talking to the pips.

He turned to look at Lisa, who was doubled up with laughter, trying to smother the laugh with a cushion.

"Oh Mr Osborne, whatever you do, don't ever change! Don't ever change!" she said, trying to catch her breath.

Chapter Thirty-eight

The excitement kept coming for Liam and Jason with the news that they had both been selected for the England U21 game against Mexico at Wembley.

"They'll have to start giving you your own peg!" joked Lisa when she heard the news. It was the third time in the last month that he would be playing at Wembley.

"You're so lucky; you know most players play their whole career without getting the opportunity." Lisa said.

Liam knew he was lucky. What he hadn't told Lisa yet was that he was also on the shortlist for the PFA Young Player of the Year. He was keeping it as a surprise as he had been allocated two tickets for the awards ceremony, and she was his plus one. Besides, even though he was only relaying news of things that were happening to him, he felt like he was boasting.

The closer the awards got, the more nervous he became. By the time he told Lisa that he had been nominated he wasn't sure he even wanted to go anymore. The ceremony was the week before the Mexico game. Liam had been more nervous about the awards ceremony than he had been the FA Cup Final. For days he had been pestering Lisa, trying everything he could to get out of it. But Lisa wouldn't let him as she saw it as a chance of getting dressed up and having a night out. Besides, she knew that he should really go, she recognised what an achievement it was. It did also mean another trek to the shops to hire a tuxedo for the night. Liam hated every moment. The last time they had gone shopping was when he had first joined the club. Lisa had kindly stepped in and helped him buy a new wardrobe. To be the part you have to look the part, she had said. That had been fun. But this time, he wasn't in the mood. Partly because he hated the idea of wearing a tuxedo and partly because they couldn't move three steps without having to sign something or have a picture taken. He felt well outside his comfort zone and was like a child being marched around a supermarket against their will. Lisa had even less fun than him, cast as the mother in the analogy. She felt like she *had* dragged him around the shops.

***

"Ah, Mr Osborne. This way please. Follow me."

Lisa giggled at the 'Mr Osborne' and received a playful elbow in the ribs for her indiscretion. They followed the waiter to their tables at the front of the room, near the stage. Liam nearly turned around and walked out when he saw who he was sitting with.

Dean Beadle had been dropped from the final squad for the European Championships. The rumours were that Howard Taylor had felt his poor attitude had a negative effect on the rest of the squad. He also had a poor disciplinary record and the English press had labelled him a loose cannon. It had been widely reported that he trashed his hotel room after he was told that he hadn't made the final twenty. Lisa took the seat next to Beadle so that Liam didn't have to. Beadle was dressed in a cream tuxedo with a red bow tie. In front of him was the biggest bottle of champagne Liam had ever seen. Sitting next to him was Linda Fox, the page three girl. Beadle was a living cliché, if he was chocolate, he would have eaten himself.

"Aye, aye, the competition's here!" said Beadle.

Liam just smiled and sat down. *Of course, Dean Beadle must also be up for the award.* Beadle had scored twenty-five goals for Tottenford and was again the leading scorer in the division.

"And I thought this couldn't get any worse," whispered Liam into Lisa's ear.

"Not that there is any competition" said Beadle to Linda Fox, just loud enough for everyone to hear.

The rest of the evening continued in the same way. If anything, the more Beadle drank, the worse it got. At first it was Lisa putting her hand on Liam's leg to calm him down after another barbed remark by Beadle. By the end of the night, it was Liam practically holding Lisa back to prevent her from launching herself across the table like a tiger going in for the kill.

Eventually, the ceremony got to the Young Player of the Year award. The five players were introduced, and a little video montage showed some of their best moments from the season. Liam's goal against Skelton got its own round of applause. It had been voted Goal of the Season and had become part of the Match of the Day opening credits. Liam sank into his chair as the video was being shown and turned a deep shade of crimson. Then, when it was Beadle's montage, Beadle whooped and clapped all his own action, pointing out details to Linda Fox, who seemed confused by the whole thing.

Then came the announcement.

"And in the tightest vote in PFA history, the winner of the PFA Young Player of the Year is… Dean Beadle."

Although Liam would have loved to have won, even if just to wipe the smug look off Beadle's face, he didn't really mind. When he had been watching his montage, other than being embarrassed, he had had a moment of clarity. Sitting there, next to the woman he loved, he had come so far. It had all happened so quickly that sometimes he forgot just what a wonderful life he was living. He even found it in his heart to feel pleased for Beadle as he stood up to get his award. That didn't last long though.

"I guess you're destined to always finish second," said Beadle behind his hand so the cameras wouldn't pick it up. "Even your bird is second best."

Liam saw red, he didn't care about the cameras. Dean Beadle was going to get what he deserved, and it wasn't going to be pretty. He was too late, though. As Beadle made his way past Lisa, Lisa slipped out her foot. Beadle stumbled forward, spilling champagne down the front of his previously spotless cream tuxedo. Liam desperately tried not to laugh, very aware of the TV cameras, which caught everything except Lisa's part in the stumble.

The sight of a seriously annoyed Dean Beadle picking up his award with a wet, discoloured tuxedo had been worth all of Liam's previous angst. When they left and the press outside wanted a picture of the two golden hopes of English football, Liam jumped at the opportunity, pulling Beadle towards him. He even asked the cameraman if he could send him a copy. There was nothing he wanted more than a memento of the night. A picture of a bristling Dean Beadle with a huge champagne stain across his £2000 tuxedo.

"I'm getting that one framed," said Liam, just loud enough for Beadle to hear as he scurried away, closely followed by Linda Fox.

"Second place never felt so sweet," said Lisa, just as loudly.

Chapter Thirty-nine

Liam was looking at the numbers of the street, trying not to appear too conspicuous. He was getting used to feeling out of place, but even for him this was tipping the scale.

Here it is, number twenty-two. Liam had travelled into West London on the Tube wearing his best suit – he only had two. Lancaster Gate was an address synonymous with English football. The whole street was like something out of a Sherlock Holmes book. The buildings were multi-storey white brick and reminded Liam of the Iranian Embassy siege when the SAS soldiers swung in through the windows on ropes. He stepped up to the door and pressed the buzzer. The letter he had received told him to be there at 1.30pm prompt. He checked his watch, 1.25pm.

Maybe I should walk around the block.

The door clicked open and Liam made his way in. Straight away he recognised most of the faces in the room. He had played against most of them over the course of the last season. Two faces stood out more than the others. The smiling, welcoming face of Jason Blackmore and the self-satisfied smug face of Dean Beadle.

Liam tried not to catch Beadle's eye and instead made his way across to Jason. Jason looked terrified and was obviously relieved to see Liam.

Liam didn't recognise the coaching staff for the U21 team, but figured that they were the group of older men dressed in matching suits standing to the side of where the players had congregated.

It wasn't long before they were given the call to make their way outside, where the coach was waiting. Liam and Jason sat next to each other in the middle of the coach. They didn't speak for the whole journey to St Albans, where they were staying for the next three nights. Nerves had taken hold.

The itinerary for the rest of the day was a bit of lunch followed by a walk around the hotel grounds. Then there was a briefing on the tactics for Sunday's game. It was clear from the talk that

Liam would be up front with Beadle, while it looked like Jason would be starting on the bench. The manager was a huge man with a thick Geordie accent. Liam vaguely recognised him. If it was who he thought, then he had been successful in the 80s with Solent FC.

"Blackie, what's his name?" whispered Liam.

"Lawrie McFadden, mate," came the whispered reply.

Liam wasn't very impressed with the briefing. There was a lot of talk about playing direct. Getting the ball in the opponent's half as quickly as possible. It sounded like both he and Beadle would be feeding off scraps. Liam spent a lot of the briefing watching Dean Beadle. Beadle had an arrogant air about him. He wore sunglasses all the way though the briefing, even though the room was quite dark. He sat at the front with his legs outstretched and his arms crossed. You didn't need to be an expert on body language to know he was even less impressed with the briefing than Liam.

Liam got the impression that Beadle was itching to say something. On the journey down, the one thing that Jason did say was that Beadle had to be on his best behaviour. Apparently, the tantrum he threw after the Brazil game had not gone down well. His relegation to the U21s had been a punishment, a test to see how he handled himself. It made Liam laugh when he thought about how proud he was to be selected for the game while Beadle was there against his wishes. It really was a funny old game.

After the briefing, the players were given their own training kit to take to their rooms. Training on Friday was at Bisham Abbey, a short drive away, and they were told that they were to be changed and on the coach for a 10.00am departure. Liam barely slept. Partly because of nerves and partly because of Jason's snoring. At one point, it was so loud Liam wasn't sure if it was Jason or a plane passing overhead.

Training started with a slow jog around the pitch and some stretches. They then started some simple passing drills. Just diagonal passes over about forty yards. You then followed your pass. Liam soon noticed that while everyone just chipped their pass, every one of Dean Beadle's passes skimmed across the ground, never rising more than a couple of inches off the floor. Straight as an arrow. Also, on the run when you followed your pass all the players had a slow jog across. Not Beadle. He had a real change of pace, accelerating across to the other side. Liam was impressed, and started doing the same thing. Liam had been used to setting the standard in training and wasn't about to let Beadle outshine him. In the end, the two of them were sprinting across, each trying to outpace the other. Their passes were crisper and sharper. Real daisy-cutters, so called because they would have taken the heads off any daisies in their way. A few of the other players tried to do the same, but their passes didn't have the same quality and would often slice off in the wrong direction. Not Liam or Beadle. Every ball hit its target like a guided missile. Now the two of them were sprinting full speed after their pass.

Next, the defenders went off with one of the coaches to work on their shape, while the attackers went with McFadden. McFadden set up a little finishing practice. Two attackers would play a one-two then pass the ball out wide to the winger. He would knock the ball out of his feet and then cross it for the two forwards to try and get on the end of the ball. Again, when Liam or Beadle passed the ball out wide, they played it with zip and pace. Their runs were perfectly timed, arriving at the near or far post just as the ball arrived. After a while, you could see that the other players were spending more time concentrating on Liam and Beadle than they were their own attempts. Liam and Beadle were putting on quite the show. It seemed like every time the cross landed at either of them, it ended up in the back of the net. Left foot, right foot, header, volley; it didn't matter, they all ended up in the same place. It was as if they were trying to outdo each other at every go. If Liam put it in the top corner, then so did Beadle. If Beadle bent it in off the post, so would Liam. It was a masterclass in finishing. Eventually, McFadden stepped in.

"Right you two, that's quite the show you're putting on. Change pairs; Liam and Dean, you go together."

You could see that neither of them was impressed. On the first one the ball went out wide and Liam made a great near-post run, but the winger took an extra touch meaning Liam was too early.

"Switch!" came the shout from behind.

Without thinking, Liam span out and arched his run back out to the far post, while Beadle darted into the now-vacant space at the near post. Beadle arrived at the same time as the ball and he despatched it neatly into the bottom corner. The two of them exchanged curious looks on the way back for their next go.

On the next turn, it was Beadle who made the near-post run. This time, the ball was slightly behind him. Liam had seen this so, instead of running to the far post, he checked his run and arrived at about the penalty spot instead. Liam expected Beadle to try some audacious effort, still trying to get the goal for himself. Instead, Beadle had seen Liam's run out of the corner of his eye. Instead of shooting, he took a little pace off the cross with the outside of his foot, diverting it into Liam's direction. Liam then volleyed the ball into the bottom corner. Just as Beadle had on the last go. And so it continued. They may have hated each other off the pitch, but on it they had an instant connection. By the end of the practice, they were just playing on instinct. It was like they were tuned into each other's wavelength. Finally, McFadden called an end to the practice. The defenders had finished ten minutes earlier and were waiting around, transfixed with the show that Liam and Beadle had been putting on. McFadden had been enjoying himself, watching the two of them work. He had been in football for more than forty years, but he had never seen anything quite like it. In the end, he had to stop to give the goalkeepers a break as it was becoming quite demoralising for them.

The practice ended with a seven-a-side game. McFadden made sure Liam and Dean were put on the same side. Once again, after about thirty minutes, he was forced to put an end to it. Beadle and Liam's team were about ten goals ahead. He didn't want to ruin the self-esteem of the other team too much.

At the end of the match, they had a cool down before departing for the hotel on the coach. On the Saturday they had a lighter session. It didn't matter what the coaching staff did, it became a private competition between Beadle and Liam. If they ran, they had to run faster than the other. If it was passing, they had to be more accurate, cleaner, crisper. If it was finishing, they had to outscore each other.

"Hey Liam, I reckon Beadle takes on more fluids than you. Reckon he's much more hydrated," joked Jason at one point.

Liam didn't laugh, instead he went and got another bottle of water from the side of the pitch.

"Jesus mate, I was only joking," laughed Jason.

The session finished earlier than Friday.

"Hey Ben, get in goal. I want to practice some freekicks," demanded Beadle of the U21 goalkeeper.

Begrudgingly, the keeper made his way into goal. Beadle scored two of his first three attempts.

"Hold up, Dean. I'll join you," said Liam.

Lawrie McFadden was pleased when the coach turned up. Ben was supposed to be playing in goal the next day. He would have a sore back the number of times he had to bend over and fish the ball out the back of the net.

***

"Hurry up Jason, I want to get to breakfast before Beadle. You know what he's like," said Liam.

"Yes mate. I know what *he's* like," said Jason, the last two days had been a nightmare for him. Liam and Beadle tried to be first to every meal, every training session, every meeting.

It was exhausting.

As they came out their room, they saw Beadle just getting into the lift. A big grin on his face as he stared down the corridor at Liam.

"Quick, the stairs," said Liam.

"See you there, save me a ringside seat," came the sarcastic reply from Jason.

Liam barely heard it; he was already opening the door to the stairs.

Chapter Forty

The game itself was being played at Leyton's ground, a fact Beadle took great delight in. If he mentioned the FA Cup final once on game day, he mentioned it a thousand times. As they walked into the reception area of the stadium, he had made a huge drama out of wanting to visit the trophy room.

"I wonder if I'll see them at the airport next year?" said Beadle as they made their way down the tunnel to the changing rooms.

"European football for a small club like this," he said as they arrived at the changing rooms.

"Imagine losing to a team in the league below you," he remarked as they made their way out onto the pitch, and so it went on.

McFadden's team talk signalled a late change of tactics. Instead of banging on about direct football, his team talk seemed to focus on getting the ball to Liam and Beadle as often as possible. Clearly, the training sessions had opened his eyes to the talent he had at his disposal.

Liam had never been so eager for a game to start. At least while they were playing, Beadle might actually shut up.

Then the game started.

It was like the World War I truce on Boxing day. Somehow, the two enemies put their differences aside for a game of football. Mexico could not live with the two of them, their clever movement, intuitive link-up play and devastating finishing.

The score was 5-0 going into the last ten minutes. Liam and Beadle had both scored two goals. Both players were on for a hattrick. Beadle was in possession and, as had been the case for most of the game, his first inclination was to look for Liam. Liam called for a pass into feet with his back to the Mexican goal. Beadle found him with a clever pass and made a run for the return. Liam looked to get it back to Beadle, but the defenders had covered the run well. Instead, Liam looked to turn. The next thing he knew, he was unceremoniously deposited on the ground by a frustrated Mexican defender. The whistle immediately blew for a free kick.

Liam and Beadle stood over the ball.

"I've got this," said Liam confidently.

"No, I've got it," said Beadle.

"You heard Lawrie in the team talk, I'm on free kicks."

"Okay," conceded Beadle. "I'll run over it and try and move the keeper, then you hit it."

The referee blew his whistle again, signalling that he was ready for the kick to be taken. Liam lined himself up as Dean made his dummy run...

Dean Beadle struck the ball, aiming to whip it around the wall. The keeper never even moved as the ball arrowed into the far top corner. Beadle was off, running to celebrate in front of the crowd behind the goal.

Liam stood there in shock.

"He got you there, mate! You got to admit it was a great strike," said Jason as he ran past Liam to celebrate with Beadle and the rest of the team.

Liam just shrugged; he wasn't going to let Beadle ruin what had been a wonderful start to his international career. He followed Jason to celebrate with the rest of the team. When he got there, the celebrating players were just breaking up and making their way back to the halfway line. Beadle saw Liam as he turned back from the crowd. He had a wry smile on his face. Liam held out his hand, deciding to be the better man.

Dean Beadle took his hand and shook it.

"Guess you really are always going to be second best," he said with a wink.

Liam couldn't help but laugh.

Chapter Forty-one

Howard Taylor must surely have regretted his decision to leave Liam and Beadle at home in England. In their three group games, Clifton drew one and lost the other two. They failed to score a single goal. Most disappointingly for Liam, Chippy didn't play a single minute in the whole tournament. The English press coverage was brutal. Taylor came in for some scathing criticism. A lot of it became quite personal, and certainly crossed a line from journalism to a personal attack. The front page of The Globe had Taylor's face superimposed over a Mr Bean photo, with the heading BUFFOON.

"Did you see The Globe this morning?" asked Lisa.

"That was vicious, he doesn't deserve that. He was only trying to protect me, and if they knew what Beadle was like, they would have left him behind too," replied Liam.

It was a Tuesday night, and Liam was taking Lisa out for dinner at a new restaurant on the edge of town. He had explained to her that maybe if they went a little further out they wouldn't get bothered as much.

"Are you sure this is the right address?" said Lisa.

"Positive, should be just around this corner. Yes, this is it?"

Lisa looked around her, they had turned into a cul-de-sac. All she could see were houses.

"Good job, Mr Osborne. Looks like you've got us lost."

Liam ignored Lisa, and he walked up to one of the houses with a sign outside it. On closer inspection, they were more like maisonettes. Each 'house' was in fact two maisonettes.

"Oy, Mr Osborne, what's going on?" said Lisa.

Liam reached into his pocket and pulled out a set of keys. He dangled them in front of her face.

"Come on then, don't you want to see our new house?"

Lisa's jaw dropped open. For once, she was lost for words. Liam watched her with a huge smile on his face. Today had taken a lot of planning, but seeing her reaction had made it all worthwhile.

"B... b... but can we, I mean, will we, I mean, we can't afford it, can we?" she finally stammered.

"Well Miss Salow, my last wage packet says we can. Harry put in a few clauses when I signed my contract that I never knew about. One of them was that if we finish in the top ten in the First Division, I get a pay rise and a bonus."

Liam's love for Clifton Rangers had been taken advantage of when he signed his first contract with the club at eighteen. Harry had not been happy about it and so had added a few clauses that he had hoped would bring to fruition.

"A pay rise? A bonus? How much?"

"Well, I'm still probably the lowest-paid player in the league, but I'm closing the gap. Say thanks to your Dad for that one. But the bonus was five grand! That means we're renting this place for now, but when all the paperwork is sorted, we can buy it. If you want..."

"If I want! Liam it's the most amazing thing ever. Now stop talking and let's get inside. I want the full tour."

She flung her arms around Liam and gave him a huge kiss.

"Alright, alright. You'll have to get off if you want the full tour."

Just one more problem, thought Liam, *now I have to tell mum I've moved out!*

Chapter Forty-two

1992-93

Negotiations went well in the off-season and Harry was able to wrap up deals for all five of Len Carlton's recommendations. Unfortunately, through a letter, he was informed that the Chairman was only going to be giving him just over £900,000 of the TV money. The letter explained that he would get all the money as promised, but not all in one amount. It would be spread over three years. Harry was fuming. His heart wanted him to pack it in, then and there. But his head told him he had to be patient. Wait it out. He had a plan, stick to it. He was getting closer and closer. The original letter that the Chairman had signed saying that he was going to get the TV money did not have a timescale on it, therefore the Chairman was not breaking any promises. Legally, there was nothing Harry could do. So instead of the £2.76 million that he had been expecting, he ended up with about one third. He still managed to bring in three players.

"So, Steve Sallis is off the cards, £1.3 million was a big outlay, but we knew what we were getting. With £900,000 we could buy his left leg and that would be it," said Harry.

"That left leg is worth about £900,000 alone. But, yes, you are correct. We cannot afford him anymore. That leaves Whelan, O'Boyle, Panton and Royston," replied Len Carlton.

In front of them they had five dossiers on Len's recommendations. Inside was all the information from Len's scouting reports, plus some notes from Harry based on his knowledge and advice from his contacts in the game. Finally, written in red on the front, under the names of those in the dossiers, were their transfer fees.

"Steve O'Boyle's a no-brainer. At sixty grand it barely touches our budget. If you're right about him then that's quite a find. He's raw but he'll be a great understudy to Ryan. We need someone, Ryan's really suffered this year, I've got serious concerns about him," said Harry. "That leaves Danny Whelan at £600,000, Ryan Royston at £450,000 and Gary Panton at £300,000. Whichever way you arrange it, Gary Panton has to be one of them. To be fair, we lack pace on the left. When Ryan Wilson knocked the ball past him and ran, Reggie couldn't live with him. It was only when Reg decided that ball or man was getting past but not both that he stopped him. But if Wilson had been braver, there would have been nothing Reg could do. Panton could play left midfield or left back. He's got a decent delivery too."

"So," Len said, "it is a straight choice between Royston and Whelan. Royston is a hell of a centre half, he costs more, but he's proven at this level. Also, Terry Johns is not as young as he once was. You are going to need to replace him some time soon. If you bring in Royston, it also means you can give young Blackmore the odd rest too."

"That *was* the plan. Royston would be perfect for that, but then Whelan would give us some steel in the centre of the park. Too many teams did a Mansford City on us last year. We're a soft touch in there. We need someone to protect Chippy a bit. You know what it's like. I bet already half the teams in the league are planning to get amongst us and rough us up a bit. Whelan takes no prisoners, and he's a big lad too. We let in a lot from set pieces last year, he would help us there as well. Tell you what, shall we just toss a coin?" laughed Harry.

Harry's eyes met Len's, he raised his eyebrows, they had to decide somehow.

Chapter Forty-three

Preseason had given a lot of cause for optimism. O'Boyle had got quite a lot of game time as Ryan's preseason had been hampered by an Achilles tendon injury. Len looked to really have come up trumps with him. Len had seen him play for Mablethorpe's youth team as a sixteen-year-old and had followed his career closely since. Mablethorpe had money trouble and released him at the end of his YTS contract. He had gone on to play for Alford City in the eighth tier of English football. Len had looked him up a couple of times, but O'Boyle hadn't even been able to get in the first team and was working at a carbon fibre factory. Then about six months ago, a contact of Len's had told him he had seen an Alford City game and that O'Boyle was playing. Apparently, he looked like he had grown a little, lost a bit of weight and was a cut above everyone else on the pitch. He also said that he was quick, "like a rat up a drainpipe" was the exact phrase. When Len got the call from Harry, Alford was his first stop. It was a bitterly cold night and Len was one of about thirty spectators. It was a Wednesday night under a set of floodlights that were barely fit for purpose. After ten minutes, Len had seen enough. He grabbed a pie and a Bovril and watched the rest of the game through the window of the clubhouse. His little black book held the evidence of the potential he had seen. He was straight on the phone to Harry at the halftime whistle. Harry was then straight on the phone to Alford, even as the game was still underway. An agreement was put in place between the two clubs. A fee of £60,000, a new set of floodlights and three bags of footballs. Harry sent the footballs the next day.

Gary Panton had also settled straight into the side. Reggie had taken him under his wing, realising that if they could strike up a partnership it could potentially add a couple more years to his career at the top level. Defensively, if there was a quick winger they would double up, Panton's speed nullifying the threat. When Reggie felt he had the winger under control, he would push Panton forward and encourage him to attack the opposition defence. This had given Clifton another string to their bow. The pace of Panton and O'Boyle had been a real threat, especially with the creative powers of Chippy and Liam. Early in preseason, Liam would often see the pass before the two new players had made the run. On many occasions, the ball would arrive with them both still on their heels. They were quickly learning that when Liam got the ball, they already needed to be on the move.

Then there was Chippy. Harry had been worried that his lack of minutes at the European championships might have had a negative effect on him. He needn't have worried. Chippy had a spring in his step from the moment he turned up for training. He had spent three weeks in the company of the best players in the country and had held his own. It had given him both a confidence and a hunger for more. There were times when he played at almost the same level as Liam. It helped that Danny Whelan's physicality meant that he had fewer defensive responsibilities and could concentrate on what he was good at. Whelan was a beast. Physically, he was intimidating. He stood at six foot two and was as strong as a bull. He could also run all day. In training he was ahead of everyone, even Liam. Even the most physical of preseason training sessions barely seemed to dampen his brow. More importantly, he knew his limits. He would win it and give it, never trying to overcomplicate things.

All in all, it was a fantastic preparation for their second season in the top division. In truth, they were still a little light in numbers, but they were in a better state than they were at this time the year before. And they had managed to finish in tenth. Hopes were high.

They were going to test those hopes pretty quickly.

The first game of the season brought the European champions to Clifton Park.

Chapter Forty-four

"We'll support you ever more,
We'll support you ever more.
Clifton Rangers, Clifton Rangers.
We'll support you ever more,
We'll support you ever more.
Clifton Rangers, Clifton Rangers,"
The chant rung out in the rafters of Clifton Park.
On the bench, Harry looked all around him.
"1978," he said.
"What?" asked Doug.
"1978, last time I heard the crowd like this at Clifton Park. The last year we won the league." Harry said.
"That's right," chimed in Alex. "You're thinking of Colney. Last home game of the season. Full house, they never let up for one minute. Constant wall of sound. Reckon you're right H, this matches it."

The scoreboard at the back of the South stand told the story. seventy-eight minutes on the clock and Clifton were winning two-nil. All the pieces had fallen into place. Mansford had no answer. Ryan Wilson had come back strong, but with Panton doubling up he had nowhere to go. Whelan and Chippy had dominated the midfield, and Terry Johns and Jason Blackmore had not given the Mansford forwards a sniff of the ball. Then there was Liam. He had been on another level, whatever Mansford did to try and stop him he found a way to conquer them. He hadn't scored, but it was his vision and technique that had put O'Boyle clean through on goal after twenty minutes. O'Boyle had been a blur as he latched onto the pass and finished without hesitation. Steve O'Boyle had had a debut to remember. His raw pace and work rate meant he never gave the Mansford defence a moment's rest. It immediately enamoured him to the Clifton faithful. He did miss a couple of chances and there were times when his first touch got away from him, but he just needed coaching. A bonus for the club was the performance of Ryan when he replaced O'Boyle after seventy minutes. Ryan slipped into the action seamlessly. It was Ryan who scored the second goal, this time from a Chippy assist. Harry was particularly pleased that Ryan had managed to get a few minutes game time and get himself on the score sheet. He had been the one worry from preseason. Ryan's body language had been poor. In the last year he had been suffering a series of niggling injuries. In the past, Ryan hadn't looked after his body, and it now seemed he was reaping what he had sown. His frustration was palpable, and Harry was worried about the repercussions of what an unhappy Ryan might be. Some things, after all, were bigger than football.

The last twelve minutes remained comfortable for Clifton. The cherry was put on the top in the eighty-third minute. It was as if Liam had just decided that it was time for him to get in on the act. Ignoring the runs of his teammates, he surged forward with the ball, bursting past a couple of tired Mansford challenges. The finish was never in any doubt. Three nil. A marker for the season had been put down, and the Clifton fans let the players know that they believed in them with another chorus.

"We'll support you ever more,
We'll support you ever more.
Clifton Rangers, Clifton Rangers.
We'll support you ever more,
We'll support you ever more.
Clifton Rangers, Clifton Rangers."

After the game, the spirits in the home changing room were high.

"Hey Jimmy, that's twenty quid you owe the club," said Reggie to the Clifton keeper.

"What you on about now grandad?"

"You were a spectator today, so you need to pay just like the rest of 'em!" came the response from Reggie.

Chapter Forty-five

The start of the season was like a dream for everyone involved with Clifton. The first game against Mansford United had set the bar for their performances and they had rarely fallen below it. It meant that by the time they got to the start of December they were just one point behind both Mansford United and Tottenford. They were the talk of the footballing world and the talk was of them as potential title challengers.

But familiar old problems were beginning to surface.

"Jesus Dave, it's like Piccadilly Circus in here," boomed Doug walking into the physio room. "How we supposed to put on a training session if they're all in here?"

Dave just shrugged. He knew it was his job to get the players back out onto the pitch, but he had a conflict of interests as he also had a duty of care. It was the same all through the leagues, an injured player was worthless. They were considered malingerers and weak. Dave was under serious pressure to get the injured players back out and onto the training field.

"Well, look, we can get Greg and Jason back out, as long as there isn't too much twisting and turning..."

"Twisting and turning? This is football not a hundred-metre dash. Just get it sorted, at this rate we won't be able to put out a team this weekend."

Doug wasn't wrong.

The squad was still just too small. It was true they had added three more bodies, but Ryan hadn't been able to play two games on the spin all season, his latest problem was an ankle injury. Now O'Boyle had pulled up with a tight hamstring. The prognosis was that he was going to be out for the next three weeks, which meant he was going to miss the whole Christmas period.

This meant that they needed Ryan to play. Harry had spoken to Dave Sheridan, and, reluctantly, they had decided to go ahead with a series of cortisone injections to get him through the flurry of games that were coming up. Although it was common practice, Harry wasn't happy with having to do it. He had heard the stories of the damage it had done to players. It was true it numbed the pain and got them through matches, but pain was there for a reason. A warning that things weren't right. Who knew the long-term damage being done? But when he heard, Ryan had insisted he have the injections as he had grown increasingly frustrated at his inability to string a series of games together. His nickname at the club was Sicknote, and he had no argument to it. He was desperate to do his bit for the club.

Ryan wasn't the only one struggling, the younger players were all suffering. Not signing Ryan Royston had meant that Jason had played every game again. He was exhausted and his body was starting to protest. He needed a rest, his body needed to recover and repair. He was his own worst enemy. His form had been so good, Clifton could not afford to be without him. The success this season had been built on their defence. Panton and Whelan had addressed their defensive weaknesses from the previous season, but it had been the form of Jason that had brought it all together. He always seemed to be in the right place at the right time. The players would tease him about the fact that he was a defender, but his kit was always clean at the end of the game. Reggie and Terry would be caked in mud, while Jason's kit was spotless. At the end of the last game, played on a quagmire of a pitch, Reggie was at him again.

"Look at you, Blackie! You look cleaner than when you started. Do you owe Johnny money? Have you promised not to get the kit too dirty?"

"Exactly," chimed in Terry. "Look at me! Don't you ever make a slide tackle?"

"If I've had to make a slide tackle mate, then I've already made a mistake," said Jason sitting down under his peg.

Jimmy Mimms looked Terry and Reggie up and down, who stood open mouthed.

"You two must have made a lot of mistakes today!"

The changing room cracked up laughing. But it was true, his performances had been flawless. Even more remarkable was the fact that it was only his second season at this level, and that he rarely played injury-free. Another area of concern was Greg Hales, they had managed to rest him for the best part of five months, including the off season, to try and get rid of his shin splints. But within three weeks, the pain was back again. He had been booked in for an operation immediately following the Christmas fixtures. They couldn't be without him before then, even as a bit-part player. In truth, he couldn't get through a full ninety minutes and rarely completed a full week of training. Lastly, there were Chippy and Liam. Like Jason, they could not be rested. Jason, Chippy and Liam were the spine of the team. Right through the middle; centre half, central midfielder and centre forward. They were the bricks that the season had been built on, but take away one of them and it all fell down. As a result, all three were on their last legs, almost playing by muscle memory.

Harry was at his wits' end. He was getting fed up with trying to manage with one arm tied behind his back. He knew what he should be doing but was unable to do it. If he had a couple more players, he could rotate the squad a little. Allow people enough time to recover from injuries properly. Instead, his squad was getting more and more tired. Then getting more and more niggly injuries. Then these niggly injuries were getting more and more serious. It was like a snowball going downhill, getting bigger and bigger.

In the end there would be a crash.

.

Chapter Forty-six

It had been Lisa and Liam's first Christmas together at their new home. It had lived up to both their expectations, despite a peculiar schedule. Liam had trained on the morning of Christmas day, so Lisa had taken the opportunity to visit her dad and exchange presents. They were then going to have another Christmas day at Liam's mum's house on the 27th. She was going to cook a proper Christmas meal, and she had got in enough snacks to feed an army. Their actual Christmas dinner, on Christmas day, had been pasta and chicken as Liam had a game on Boxing day. They finished the day by being in bed by ten. Liam knew that Lisa was a keeper as she took the whole day in her stride. She never complained once. She didn't tell Liam but, as a Clifton fan, she felt some responsibility to ensure that Liam was at his best on Boxing day. At one point she even snatched a mince pie out of his hand, telling him he could wait until after the game.

It was a good job that he enjoyed his Christmas at the house so much as it wasn't such a great time for Clifton. Liam's performances stayed at his usual high standards, but the flurry of fixtures was just too much for the paper-thin squad they had. They picked up just one point from their three league games. It meant that, going into the new year, Clifton had fallen out of the top five for the first time that season.

The next game was a welcome break from their league form. They were playing Northwich in the cup at home. It was to be a low point in the season, despite a 2-0 victory taking them through to the fourth round.

Ryan had been having the cortisone injections throughout the Christmas period. He had been managing to get through the games but, not surprisingly, his form was poor. Harry had no choice but to keep playing him as Steve O'Boyle had been unavailable due to his hamstring injury. O'Boyle's recovery had been quicker than expected and he was back in the squad. He wasn't yet match fit so he started the game as substitute.

The cortisone injections were no longer having the full effect on Ryan, and you could see him grimace every time he tried to push off and start to run. The other players could see this and only played the ball in his direction when he was in a lot of space and always to his feet. To the crowd, it seemed as if they didn't trust Ryan and this just added fuel to the fire. They, of course, didn't know he was injured, or that he had been taking injections just to get through matches; trying not to let down his team. The fans started to get on his back. It had started earlier in the season. Ryan had missed a lot of preseason and had never really got up to match sharpness. It began with a few disgruntled mumbles from the terraces. Then there had been a few unflattering articles in the club fanzine. Now it had become full-blown hostility. The fans had taken to O'Boyle, he was keen and full of energy. He was a chaser of lost causes; they could identify with him. But as far as the fans could see Ryan wasn't trying, they thought he was lazy. Every time the ball went in his direction you could hear the crowd react. The other players felt sorry for him. They knew his full story. They knew he was sacrificing himself for the team. The worse it got, the worse Ryan played. He was overthinking everything. He was desperate to do well, to show everyone that he was trying his best, but it meant that when he got the ball, he wasn't relaxed. Balls bounced off him, passes went astray. With every mistake, the discontent from the crowd became greater. At one point O'Boyle went to warm up and the whole crowd cheered and applauded him. In the end, Harry took Ryan off for his own protection. When Ryan's number was raised the crowd actually cheered. He looked like he had the weight of the world on his shoulders as he left the field. O'Boyle took his place and sprinted onto the pitch full of energy, a contrast to the dejected figure that he had replaced.

A despondent Ryan slumped onto the bench. His ankle was throbbing, and he could barely watch. To rub salt in his wounds both Rangers' goals came from the fresh legs of O'Boyle. The cheers of the Rangers' crowd were like daggers to Ryan's heart.

**

"How's Ryan?" said Lisa to Liam as he entered the players' lounge.

"Not good, he just shot off. We all tried to gee him up, let him know that he was important to the team. To us. But he barely acknowledged us. I'm worried about him. I don't *think* he's drinking, but I'm not sure. I know what it's like, Lisa. I've seen it with my own eyes as a kid. You can't just switch it on and off. It stays with you forever. I just hope that having Mary and the kids with him will help him stay strong. He's pulling away from us all, it's been happening all season."

"Liam, it was terrible. I've never known the fans to turn on a player like that. Even in the bad days of relegation. I felt embarrassed to be a Rangers fan, and I've never felt like that."

"I just hope he's gone straight home."

Chapter Forty-seven

The next two months were full of inconsistencies. Ryan was no longer a starter, instead Steve O'Boyle had become the team's number nine. To Harry, it felt like he had given in to the pressure from the crowd, but he knew that the state Ryan was in, both physically and mentally, he couldn't justify starting him. It may have been what the crowd wanted but O'Boyle, or Boyley as he had become known, was still young and inexperienced. His performance fluctuated from game to game, sometimes from minute to minute. With a fit Ryan, the club had an experienced player who knew what his role was. He made the right runs and invariably made the right choices. With Boyley, there were times when his own teammates didn't know what he was going to do. There were times when it looked like he didn't know what he was going to do. But he scored goals. Including the two goals in the FA Cup, he had scored seven goals in eleven games. In those eleven games Clifton had won five, drawn two and lost four. Three of those victories had come in the FA Cup. Like the previous season, the FA Cup draws had been kind to Clifton; they were yet to play a team from the First Division. It meant that while they were now down in eighth place, they were through to the quarter finals for the second consecutive season. Despite this, there was an air of disappointment at the club. The start to the season had held so much promise, and the team genuinely felt that they had the ability to still be challenging at the top of the division. Once again, it was the same old story. The lack of real investment was dragging them down. The squad had been overused and, as a result, even in eighth place, they were looking over their shoulder rather than chasing the teams above.

It was no coincidence that the two victories in the league had come when Harry had an almost fully fit squad. The players were frustrated, the fans were frustrated and so were the coaching staff. At the start of the season, the training ground and the stadium had been fun places to be, full of banter and optimism. Now it was different, it had become a struggle. A struggle for form, and a struggle for consistency. The team felt that every time they made a step forward, they then took two back. There was nothing worse than losing to teams you knew you would beat if only you were given a fair chance. An even playing field.

"You know what Clem, I'm not sure I can do this much longer. It feels like the wheels have come off. I don't think I can work in a place where we aren't all pulling in the same direction," said Harry one day at training.

"I get what you're saying Harry, but we've still got a lot to play for. I look at the players we have, and I know we're *so* close. If we just had a couple more bodies, who knows where we'd be," said Doug.

"Exactly, I feel like this should be our time. If the Chairman had given me the money he promised, I honestly feel like we could've challenged this year. He's played me for a fool. I've got to tell you Clem, I've written out a letter of resignation. I've even printed it out. It's in my drawer. If I didn't feel like I owe it to this set of players to see this through to the end, I'd already be gone. The thing is, I can't see the end anymore. I want this club back where it belongs, at the very highest echelons. But, with him as Chairman, it's never going to happen. I don't think I can wait any longer."

"Well, look, we've got the quarter finals up next. That's three wins away from a major trophy, then European football. That's not standing still. If we stay up, he'll have to give you next year's TV money and the rest of the cash from this year. That's a tidy lump. Think what you can do with that."

"If you think he's going to let that happen, then you're a bigger fool than me Clem."

Chapter Forty-eight

Before the quarter final, a couple of hours before training was due to begin, Harry received a visit from a serious Ryan.

"Hi gaffer, is it alright if I have a word?"

"Of course, Ryan, you know my office is always open to you."

"This is so difficult for me, after all you did for me a couple of years ago. I don't think I'd even be standing here today if it weren't for you," he paused, took a deep breath as he tried to control his emotions. "I'm done Boss. You know after the game last week, I went straight to one of my old haunts, The Black Bear. I sat there for an hour with a whisky, just looking at it. I've never wanted a drink so much in my life. But I didn't drink it. I can't say with any certainty that next time I won't. I hate to ask, but I need your help again."

Harry nodded his head, "Of course Ryan, you know me. Some things are more important than football."

"First of all, I want to stop the injections. They're doing me no good. I want to have a complete break. Let my body heal itself. I know we're short of players, but I've been going from one injury to another for the best part of a year and a half now. I don't blame the fans digging me out, I can't remember the last time I was fully fit and performing to the level I should be. I honestly think it's Karma for all those years I didn't care. Back then I never had so much as an ingrowing toenail, now I can't catch a break. I've spoken to Mary; we both feel I need a complete change. Get away from my past."

Harry just stood there, nodding. He knew they were already struggling to put out a side, but he was being honest when he said some things were bigger than football. He had seen the life that Ryan had been living, and he considered the progress Ryan had made as one of his biggest successes in football.

Nearly two hours later, when they had fully discussed everything, they shook hands and together went out to talk to the rest of the squad.

"Right lads, team meeting in the changing room, everyone in now." The booming voice of Doug brought everyone running. Liam gave Jason a curious look. Ryan had been conspicuous by his absence. They weren't expecting good news. "Right boys, I'm not going to keep you in the dark for a second longer. I'm going to pass straight over to Ryan and let him explain," with that Harry took a seat alongside the players and Ryan stepped forward.

"Okay, I don't want to take up any more of your precious time than I need to. I just wanted to say that I love this club, and I love every one of you. You've all been there for me, and I can't thank you enough. I'm fully committed to the Clifton cause, but you all know I've been struggling. You would have to be blind not to have seen it. I've spoken to the gaffer, and I want you all to know that this'll be my last season at Clifton. My last season as a professional footballer. I'm retiring at the end of the season. My body's been telling me that it's time for quite a while now. I've been trying to ignore it, but I feel like I'm doing you and me a disservice if I don't do this. I will be seeing out the season and I promise that I won't be the miserable git I've become recently."

A lot of the players laughed at this last comment, and the tension in the room dissipated slightly.

"Recently? You've always been a miserable git," quipped Jimmy Mimms.

"Some of your performances, maybe it should be a joint retirement laddie," said Ryan, a smile appearing on his face for what seemed like the first time in months.

The meeting then descended into various insults alongside best wishes being offered to Ryan on his decision.

"Right you lot, no one's retired yet. So, get your backsides out on that pitch. We have a quarter final to win at the weekend!" shouted Doug.

The players all left, leaving Ryan alone with Harry again.

"I've been thinking," said Harry. "If you're serious about a new start, I might have something that's right up your street."

Chapter Forty-nine

The squad for the quarter final included three youth team players. Harry had been tempted to include Alex again, but after the last game he had barely been able to walk for weeks. The players had bought him a Zimmer frame and brought it out to training. Alex had used it for the session, only half-joking.

Clifton's good fortune in the cup had started to be commented on. Once again, the phrase "name is on the cup" was being bandied about. The quarter final against Hullingborough was another close game, despite the gap in stature. In the end, it was an unlikely source that saw them progress through to the semi-finals.

"Chippy, feet," shouted Liam.

Liam checked his run, receiving the pass from Chippy in a rare bit of space. Many teams had tried to man-mark Liam, feeling that he was Clifton's main threat, but few had managed to curtail him for the whole game. His marker had been getting more and more desperate as he felt Liam's influence growing. This time he launched himself in on the challenge, trying desperately to stop Liam before he got any momentum.

He was too late.

Liam saw him coming and comfortably hurdled the challenge. He was out wide and near the touchline, the Hullingborough fullback charging out of position, aware of the danger that Liam posed. But Liam was one step ahead. He pushed the ball past the defender into the open spaces and sprinted after it. Hullingborough were frantically back peddling, their centre half had to come out wide to challenge Liam. Again, Liam just poked the ball past him and, with a quick change of pace, left the defender behind. Liam was now too wide to threaten the goal himself. Instead, he floated the ball up to the far post, hoping that someone was attacking the space. Scott Fulling arrived at the same time as the ball. It was not a conventional header, it seemed to almost hit him on the head. But it did the job. Scott was immediately off running around the track. He had taken his shirt of and was whirling it around his head. He was never one for a subtle celebration. The players had to practically drag him to the ground to stop him. In the changing room afterwards, some of the players joked that it was the longest run they had seen him make.

They were now set for a return to the twin towers on the 3rd of April. It was Scott's first goal since his winner against Thamesmead in the previous year's run to the final. This time, he had even known what he was doing. The players and the fans took this as a good sign.

Could this be their year?

A week after the Hullingborough game, England lost 2-0 at home to a strong Dutch side. The 2-0 score line had flattered England, they had been completely outclassed. The second goal, scored by reigning European footballer of the year Rudd Hendrix, came at the end of a thirty-eight-pass move. Hendrix, along with his SS Milan teammates Marco Van Den Berg and Frank Bakker, dominated the game to pile even more pressure on under-fire Boss Howard Taylor. The Globe had started a campaign to get rid of Taylor, they argued that he was scared to ring the changes. That he needed to take the country forward. That he needed to put his faith in the new generation. That he needed to call up Liam Osborne and Dean Beadle.

The day after the game, Liam received a phone call.

Chapter Fifty

The clamour for Liam and Beadle to be brought into the England squad gathered momentum as March progressed. Liam's form did nothing to slow the momentum as he continued to put in man-of-the-match performances even in a team that was well below strength. Ryan had not played in any games since his announcement. Harry had been true to his word and Ryan had spent the time getting injury free and was now starting to build up his own fitness. Dave Sheridan had put together a rehabilitation programme that finished with Ryan having to do another preseason style campaign of fitness work. Ryan hadn't moaned once, instead he had been almost chirpy by his standards. You could tell that a weight had been lifted from him and he looked eager to return. It had helped that "someone" had leaked the fact that Ryan had been playing injured for much of the season out of his love for the club. The source inside the club had gone on to say that Ryan was one of the hardest working, most respected players at the club.

After their final league game in March, the England squad for the group game against San Marino was announced. It was a great day for Clifton and for Liam as he, Chippy and Jason were all drafted into the squad. It was the first time since 1979 that there had been three Clifton players representing their country. It had not been a surprise for Liam; Howard Taylor had told him he was in the squad immediately following the Dutch debacle. The Globe newspaper took the credit for not only Liam's inclusion but also that of Dean Beadle.

The experience with the senior squad was remarkably like the one Liam had had with the U21s, even down to his competitiveness with Beadle. The senior players did not know what to make of it. Jason, on the other hand, spent the whole time with a knowing smile on his face. He was the least phased player there. Normally, young players blended into the background, trying not to get noticed too much. In his whole life, Dean Beadle had never blended in, whereas Liam was too wrapped up with his battle with Beadle to give it a second thought. Despite neither of them having reached their twenty-second birthday, they were both the best players in every session that Howard Taylor and his coaching staff put on. Jason and Chippy both performed well, too. Having all three of them there was like having a security blanket. You could tell they were all having the time of their lives. When the team was announced, it was a surprise that Liam was only a substitute. Even the older players had expected him to be starting after his form in training. Chippy was on the bench with Liam, he had spent the majority of his England career there.

Jason Blackmore had always been in Liam's shadow. When Liam had joined Clifton Rangers, he had soon replaced Jason as the best young prospect at the club. Liam's incredible rise had always meant that Jason seemed like an afterthought, a footnote. In a strange way, Liam felt almost happier than he would have done if it had been him starting his first game for his country. Liam would never forget the support Jason had given him, at a time when he needed it the most. Jason was one of those people who made everyone around him feel at ease. Jason making his full debut for England was celebrated by everyone who had crossed his path.

"Even second best at your club."

Dean Beadle never missed an opportunity to needle Liam.

They were waiting in the lobby for the coach to take them to the stadium. Beadle was once again wearing sunglasses indoors and bowling about the place like he owned it. This was also to be his start for England. It was fair to say that everyone who had crossed his path would not be celebrating the news.

"Never happier to be second, never happier," said Liam, patting Jason on the back.

Liam tried to take in every moment of the day. His mum and Uncle Gary were both there to watch, as were Harry and Len Carlton. It was a proud moment for all of them. The proudest person in the stadium that day, though, was Lisa. Since moving in together the bond they shared had grown and grown. By the time she took her seat, she was an emotional wreck. She had seen what it meant to Liam, and she knew the sacrifices he had made to get to this moment.

As much as Liam was loving the whole experience, when the teams lined up and the national anthems played, he wished he was starting the game. Training over the last few days had shown him that he did belong at this level, and he was itching to show the world what he could do. He didn't allow himself to be dispirited, though. When he had first joined Clifton as a seventeen-year-old he had spent many games as a substitute. In the end, he had turned it to his advantage. He had learned to study the other team's tactics and formation; looking for weaknesses to exploit.

The first weakness he spotted was in his own team. Almost directly from kick-off, Jason's partner at centre half under hit a back pass to the goalkeeper. The San Marino striker looked as surprised as everyone in the stadium as he latched onto the ball and slipped it past the England goalkeeper. The whole stadium was silent except for the typing of journalists already writing Taylor's obituary. This was the same San Marino team that had let in nine goals against the Netherlands.

Many of the members of the press section were probably disappointed with the rest of the match, although they did get their story.

The three Clifton players had a mixed night. Disappointingly, Chippy remained an unused substitute. Jason played the full ninety minutes and he would tell his dad after the game that he could have borrowed his pipe and slippers, he had so little to do. In fact, other than the goal in the first minute, the San Marino team rarely ventured out of the security of their own half. Security wasn't the best word as the San Marino defence was breeched seven times in the eighty-nine minutes that followed. With the score at 4-1, Liam was sent to warm up. By the time he was called back and his number held up, the score was 5-1. He didn't care. As he entered the field, he bent down and touched the hallowed Wembley turf. Most people never live their dreams, they stay locked away and untouched. Life is something that happens to them while they're dreaming. For Liam, his dreams and his life regularly merged. Today was literally a dream he had had since the age of five. The circumstances were always different. Brazil at the Maracanã, Scotland, the auld enemy at Hampden, sometimes it was a World Cup Final, sometimes the opposition was unknown, but always he had reached down and touched the grass. He looked up to the skies, he didn't believe in God but if there was one, today he was looking out for Liam.

"Wake up, Silver! Watch closely, you might learn something."

Beadle woke Liam from his moment with his usual tact and consideration.

Even you can't spoil this moment, thought Liam.

There was still twenty-five minutes to go and it was one-way traffic. The San Marino defence were now camped deep in their half. They no longer even left a player forward. Therefore, whenever they cleared it, the ball just came straight back at them. Beadle had already scored twice and was desperate to complete his hattrick. Playing against a packed defence is never easy. The phrase park the bus was not yet a thing, but if it was this San Marino team had used a double decker. Immediately, the understanding between Beadle and Liam was evident. Within a minute of coming on, only a last-ditch tackle prevented the two of them combining for another Beadle goal. Five minutes later, they were unstoppable. In a dazzling display of one-touch pass and move, the two young English forwards sliced their way through the San Marino ranks. The final pass from Liam had tempted the San Marino keeper from his line. Beadle barely looked up. Spotting the keeper advancing out of the corner of his eye, he scooped the ball up and beyond the keeper's flailing arms. 6-1 and Beadle had completed his first international hattrick. Many players would have turned to celebrate with the player who had assisted him for the goal. Not Beadle. He was standing in front of the English supporters, arms crossed and a nodding head suggesting he had proven something to someone. In a relatively short period of time, Beadle had managed to alienate himself from most of the Premier League players, and his celebration was noticeable for the fact that it was a solo performance. Liam came closest to joining the celebration with an awkward pat on the back before returning to the halfway line ready for kick off. The referee had to practically force Beadle out of his pose so the game could continue.

Liam had never put a huge importance on personal glory. He had always been equally happy scoring or assisting; if his team got the goal then he was happy. The thing was, in his dreams, no matter whether Brazil at the Maracanã, Scotland at Hampden or, as it was on one occasion, the cast of Space Jam in a cartoon stadium, his England debut always had a goal for him. Time was slowly running out...

Liam could see that the San Marino players were now just waiting for the final whistle. In their minds, the goal in the first minute was victory enough for them. This was a team of postmen and factory workers, sharing a pitch with players they only ever read about in the San Marino equivalent of Shoot or Match magazine.

One almighty clearance from the San Marino goalkeeper had made its way through to the England keeper. The crowd had given it a sarcastic "Oooh" as if it had been a shot on target. Liam had been waiting for this moment. Twice in the first half the San Marino centre half had ducked under a long goal kick, allowing the ball to run through to his goalkeeper. By the look on his face, Liam could tell he was incredibly pleased with his cleverness each time he had done it. Liam pulled away slightly to the wing as if he was not interested and to keep out of the sight line of the defender. As the ball was kicked, he was off. With a smile on his face, the centre half once again ducked allowing the ball to continue all the way through to his keeper.

His smile soon disappeared.

Liam could see the ball arrowing down through the sky. He knew that if he let it bounce, then he had no chance of getting it before the San Marino keeper. Sprinting at full speed, he stretched out his leg to control the ball. He connected just as the ball struck the floor but before it could rebound back up again. The bottom of his studs cushioned the ball and slowed it almost to a halt. The touch reverberated through his knee, like a tiny electric shock.

Liam was clean through on goal.

His next touch brought the ball back in his path, five yards outside the area, slightly to the right-hand side, the stab of pain forgotten. The keeper came rushing out of his goal. Liam already knew what he was going to do. He had seen the goalkeeper commit himself early several times in the first sixty-five minutes. He had got away with it on a few occasions, but Liam had realised that he went down far too early. All he had to do was lift the ball over him and it was a certain goal.

"Your left, PASS!"

The shout came from just behind Liam's left shoulder. Instinctively, he faked to shoot and, as the keeper slid out, he instead rolled the ball past the keeper, to the onrushing English player. It was the easiest task for them to roll the ball into the now-empty net. The folded arms and nodding head gave away the identity of the receiver of this gift.

The typewriters started again. The press had their story, England had its hero and Liam's dream now had an edited version.

This time the whole team did celebrate. To a man, they rushed over and shook Liam's hand, patted him on the back and offered their congratulations. At least Liam had his own victory of sorts. Meanwhile, Beadle celebrated alone, seeming to neither notice nor care.

At the end of the game, when Liam finally made his way out the stadium, his welcome from Lisa was all that he needed. She rushed forward, tears in her eyes and swamped him in an embrace.

"Oh, Mr Osborne, I'm so proud of you."

Sometimes real-life can still come up trumps.

Chapter Fifty-one

It was only a four-day turnover from the San Marino game to the FA Cup Semi-Final. Harry had been pleased with how the England game had gone for all three of his players. Jason had barely needed to break into a sweat, Chippy had spent the day sitting on his behind and Liam had only played twenty-five minutes. It did make him very aware that if the three of them started being selected, and playing, more regularly, then his small squad would become even more stretched. What worried him the most was what happened when you stretched something too far. But he was encouraged by the fact that Ryan had been declared fit and was ready for a place on the bench. This meant that he had a full squad to pick from. If Clifton won, it would be only the third time in FA Cup history that a team had reached the final without playing a team from the top division. It was almost as if they were fated to get to their second consecutive final.

Millham were runaway leaders of the championship, they were eight points clear of second place and eleven clear of third. Promotion was a certainty. For them there was nothing to lose. Reaching the semi-final had been a great achievement. In contrast to Clifton, they had already knocked two Premiership sides out of the competition. Including, in the last round, one of the biggest shocks in history by knocking out Tottenford. In many people's eyes, Clifton went into the game as underdogs. That suited Harry.

"Look boys, last year we struggled when Leyton just sat back and defended. I don't expect this lot to do that. I know Tottenford rested a few, but Millham really went at them. I look at our team today and I know we're a match for anyone. These will let us play, and there will be spaces to exploit. Do your jobs defensively, but when you get the ball, enjoy yourself."

The reaction from the players was positive, lots of nodding heads and affirmative mutterings. They knew what they were capable of when they could field their best team. Every player knew they could trust the player sitting next to them. They were determined that today wasn't going to be another Leyton.

The first ten minutes were a battle, both teams were up for the game and the tackles were flying in. When the game settled down it soon became clear that Clifton were the better side, and they had the greater quality. The three players just back from England duty brought with them a confidence and swagger that was infectious. Jason marshalled the defence, even telling Terry Johns what to do and where to go. Terry felt like telling Jason where to go too, but in his heart, he knew that it was a positive thing. The extra communication from Jason made Terry's job easier and the whole Clifton defence looked solid as a result. In midfield, Chippy was pulling all the strings, Danny Whelan gave them legs and aggression while Chippy gave them quality. The Millham players couldn't get near him, he always seemed to have time on the ball and be one step ahead. It seemed like a case of when and not if Clifton were going to take the lead. Then up front there was Liam, whose debut for England seemed to have lifted him to even greater heights. He was mesmerising to watch, every time he got the ball, he made something happen. The Millham defence looked terrified of him.

"H, Boyley is trying to signal you something," said Alex, pointing in O'Boyle's direction.

Steve O'Boyle was pointing to his hamstring and pushing his fists together. He had a grimace on his face.

Reggie was the closest player to the bench, "It's his hamstring Boss, he says it's tight."

Harry looked around him at the players on the bench.

"Ryan, go get warmed up, he's coming off, we can't risk him tearing it," he then turned back to Reggie. "Get him to go down, we'll get Dave on to have a look."

Dave just confirmed what Harry had thought.

As Ryan took his place on the field, the reaction of the crowd seemed positive and he got a generous round of applause. Harry's public relations had obviously done their job. If anything, the introduction of Ryan gave Clifton another boost. He looked fresh and hungry for the ball. O'Boyle was a bit of a wildcard capable of moments of brilliance, but his decision making was still inconsistent. With Ryan, they had a more well-rounded player who linked the game together. Ryan looked like he was enjoying himself, and with Liam and Chippy on top of their games you sensed it wouldn't be long before he would have a chance to do what he did best. Even at his lowest point, Ryan McLoughlin had always had an eye for a goal.

With halftime approaching, once again the ball found its way to Liam. The Millham defence sat off nervously. They had been incapable of dealing with him, and hesitated closing him down. That was all that Liam and Ryan needed. Ryan set off, he knew that Liam having time and space meant one thing. If Ryan could make a good run, Liam would find him. The pass was perfect, bisecting the two central defenders straight into Ryan's path. Ryan rounded the Millham keeper like a matador side-stepping a bull. The floundering, desperate keeper clawed at the ball but missed it, catching Ryan instead. He tumbled to the floor. The crowd held their breath. The referee blew his whistle. It was a penalty to Clifton. But who was going to take it?

Ryan carefully picked up the ball as he rose to his feet, like a bomb disposal expert lifting a suspicious package.

"I'll have it Ryan," said the oncoming Liam. Only too aware that it was the same end, the same goal that Ryan had missed the game-changing penalty in last year's final.

"No laddie, there's only one person taking this," said Ryan. "And you're talking to him."

The Millham players did not even argue, the only question was whether the keeper would be sent off. The keeper was truly fortunate, the referee perhaps considering the occasion rather than strictly following the laws of the game. Whatever the reason, he only received a yellow card. Twice in as many years Clifton had been on the wrong side of a lenient referee.

Ryan placed the ball carefully on the spot and paced out his run up. He took a deep breath, settled himself and decided where he was going to put the ball. The referee blew his whistle and Ryan stepped forward. He struck the ball sweetly, aiming towards the same corner as the penalty he missed in the previous year's final. The keeper guessed right and was already on his way. This time, though, the ball was struck too well. It nestled in the back of the net before the keeper could get anywhere near it.

The flood of emotion that emitted from Ryan was primal in its nature. He stood there, fists clenched, the veins in his neck throbbing. An unintelligible scream banishing his demons once and for all. It was an image that was to go down in Clifton Rangers' folklore.

The second half was no different from the first. The gulf in class was clear. All that was left was the familiar cherry on top.

As much as Clifton were the better side, it was an uneasy nervousness that had come over them and the crowd. As long as the game stayed at 1-0, Millham always had a chance. Liam knew that a second goal would settle the nerves and finish the game as a contest. He decided to take the matter into his own hands.

A crunching tackle from Whelan gained possession for Clifton and the ball was quickly moved onto Liam via Chippy. As before, Ryan set off while the Millham players backed away. This time, though, Liam wasn't looking for his strike partner. This time he was going it alone. He glided this way and that like a slalom skier dodging in and out of the gates while traversing the snow and ice. But instead of gates, it was Millham players who were left in his wake. The final defender was used merely as a wall to block the keeper's view as Liam bent it around him and into the far corner. He didn't stop running, sliding on his knees towards the Clifton fans behind the goal. He was soon buried underneath an avalanche of Clifton players. They were back in the final.

When Liam finally managed to get up from the floor, he looked for Lisa in the crowd, he knew roughly where she was and waved in her direction. As he jogged back to the halfway line, he took a sharp intake of breath. He flexed his knee. It was the same knee he had felt on England duty. It had locked on him for a fraction of a second, giving a sharp, shooting pain. The game soon finished, and the team did a slow lap of the famous old pitch taking in the crowd's congratulations, savouring every moment. Liam walked at the back. On a day where he had put in the perfect performance, his worst decision had ended up being his choice of celebration.

Chapter Fifty-two

"That's not good Liam, you need to ring Dave."

Lisa was talking about Liam's knee. Overnight, it had swollen to the size of a beehive. He could put weight on it, but could barely bend it. Liam still didn't drive so he rang his Uncle Gary who gave him and Lisa a lift to Clifton Park. It was Sunday and, other than Dave Sheridan, the cleaners and Ken the groundsman, the stadium was empty.

"Thanks Gaz," said Liam as Lisa helped him from the car. The seat was pushed right back as Liam still couldn't bend his knee properly.

Dave took one look at it and sent him back home again.

"It's too swollen to see what's wrong at this stage, Liam. You need to ice it, and keep it raised above your heart. In a few days, when it's gone down, we'll have another look. Sometimes you can just tweak a ligament and it swells up to protect it. You might be lucky. If it's no better, we'll get an x-ray. But again, you can't x-ray it all swollen like that."

He gave Liam a pile of anti-inflammatory tablets to take and told him to stay off his knee for the next few days.

***

Lisa loved Liam deeply, but she had never been so relieved in all her life when he was given the OK to go into the training ground for treatment and give her some peace. Lisa had made sure that Liam did exactly what Dave had told him to. This meant that she set him up in the living room with a pile of pillows under his leg. She also went to the local shop and bought three bags of frozen peas, which she then rotated to make sure that he always had freezing cold ice on his knee. Unfortunately, without football, Liam was unbearable. He sulked from the moment Dave told him to go home and rest until the moment his knee was normal enough to return to the club. Three days Lisa had to run around after him. Three days, no matter what she did she couldn't get a smile on his face. She tried to spoil him. She bought him magazines and sweets and videos but still he looked like a five-year-old who has dropped his ice cream. By day two, Liam had taken to ringing her when he wanted something.

She was still in the house, but he was ringing her.

Every ten minutes.

"Can you get me a sandwich?"

"My ice needs changing."

"Can you change the video?"

By the third day she was close to sticking his phone in a rather uncomfortable place.

She did understand, though.

On Wednesday, Clifton Lost 2-0, Liam couldn't even watch the game. On Thursday, he returned to the training ground. Dave pulled his knee about a bit, much to Liam's discomfort.

"Feels okay, but it's still a bit swollen. We'll put you on the suckers and give you some ultrasound over the next couple of days. That should get rid of it. Then, hopefully, you can do some light training early next week."

"Early next week, then I could be back for the Richmond game on Tuesday?" asked Liam.

"Liam, knees are unpredictable things. Honestly, realistically, Tuesday's too soon. I would say you have an outside chance for next Saturday. But the Chorley game the following Saturday sounds more likely."

Liam didn't travel with the team to Richmond as they thought it was a bit much for him. Instead, the club issued him with crutches and told him not to put any weight on his leg. Lisa and Liam listened to the game on the radio instead. It didn't help Liam's mood when they lost 3-1.

"At least it shows they're missing you," tried Lisa.

"Hmmph," was the reply.

Lisa started to wonder if you could get divorced before you get married.

Liam watched the Tuesday game at Clifton Park. During the day, he had managed to do some light jogging in straight lines and hadn't had any adverse reaction. He was still hoping to play a part on the coming Saturday. It was true that the league matches meant little. Clifton were firmly placed in the middle of the table. They were in no danger of relegation, but they were also in no danger of going much higher. But Liam lived for his football, if he was playing, everything else in his life seemed to fit into place and make sense to him. Without it, he was lost. Secondly, the next England squad was due to be announced after Saturday's game. Liam knew that if he wasn't playing, then he wouldn't be picked. The speculation in the papers was that Liam was going to be handed his full debut - if he was fit. His mood wasn't improved when Clifton were beaten 3-2 by lowly Richmond.

Liam was the only player in training on Wednesday, everyone else was given a day off. This was normal practice for the day following a game. To be fit for Saturday, he knew that he would need to be able to join in with full training on Thursday and Friday. He hadn't kicked a ball since the semi-final. The swelling had all gone and left in its place was a huge yellow and purple bruise that even spread into his thigh. Dave Sheridan had assured him that this was normal.

"Can I kick a ball yet Dave?" asked Liam.

"If you want my honest opinion, I wouldn't yet. Another week and you'll be back to one hundred per cent, but I know that's not what you want to hear. We can give it a go, but I warn you it may set your recovery back a bit."

"Okay, fair enough. I still want to give it a go though," said Liam.

"Okay, we'll try a few quicker runs and changes of direction. Then if that goes okay, we'll try you out with a ball. It's the only way to know for sure."

Dave put out some cones in two parallel lines.

"To start with, just jog from one side to the other," said Dave.

Liam felt rather good.

"Right, now, as you turn at each cone, just push off for a few yards. A little change of pace."

Liam could just feel his knee a little as he pushed off but by the time he got to the end, it felt okay.

"I could feel it a little at the start," he called to Dave as he made his way back to the beginning.

"You will feel a little discomfort, you haven't used it for a week and a half, it's still a bit tender, too. On this next set, I want you to stay facing forwards and push off to the side at each cone."

The first time Liam pushed off from the cone, he felt a sharp pain down the inside of his knee. Again, though, by the time he got to the end it had felt more or less normal. He didn't mention it to Dave this time.

Dave then grabbed the ball he had brought out with him.

"Now for the real test," he said. "First of all, just little side foot volleys, then we'll go onto laces."

The first few side foot volleys jolted his knee a little, but the laces volleys felt fine.

"Okay, now just some side foot passing."

When he stood there and had time to prepare himself, Liam was fine. But then Dave started passing the ball to the side of Liam. Liam's knee felt weak each time he tried to pass the ball while on the move. He couldn't really get any crispness in his passing. Dave saw it straight away.

"Right stop, you're not ready Liam. You've made great progress and you aren't far away, but there's no way you're ready to join back in training tomorrow. Saturday's just too soon for you. If you listen to me and do things properly, then you'll be back for the following Saturday. The 21st against Chorley."

Liam's heart sank. He knew Dave was right, but the England squad was being announced on the 19th. He now knew it wouldn't include him.

Thursday morning, Liam's knee was extremely sore from the previous day's exertion. Dave was now not sure that Liam would even be ready for Chorley on the 21st.

Lisa took the news as badly as Liam. The honeymoon period was well and truly over. Liam was like Jekyll and Hyde. When he was playing football and things were going well, he was almost the perfect man. But over the last two weeks, Mr Hyde had shown his face. There was no reasoning with him. Lisa tried to talk him round, but he had lost all perspective. She told him that at least it wasn't a serious injury. She tried to explain to him that the cup final was the thing he should focus on. She told him that he would soon be back playing again. In the end, Lisa found that the best thing to do was just stay out of his way.

On Saturday, Clifton picked up their first point since Liam's injury. Liam finally joined in training on the following Thursday. It was far from his best training session. He was rusty and off the pace. Although he was disappointed with his performance, he was pleased to be back. He was also happy to see that Jason and

Chippy had been named in the England squad for the qualifier against Norway. It was a big game for England. If they lost, then they couldn't qualify. Even a draw might not be enough. Once again, the heat was being turned up on Howard Taylor.

Liam was called into Harry's office after training on Friday. Again, Liam had not been at his best.

"How's it feeling Liam?" said Harry.

"The knee feels fine Boss, but I just feel nervous. It's like pulling off a plaster. Every time I go to change direction quickly or strike the ball, I flinch and don't quite do it at full power. I'm waiting for a pain that never comes. It's so frustrating."

"Liam, you're going to have a long career in this game. In football terms, you're still a baby. Most players don't even get into the first team by your age. You'll get injuries, they're frustrating. But you can't rush them. You must go through the process and listen to your body. After Saturday's game, we've ten days because of the international break. Then there's two more games until the final. I'm putting you on the bench Saturday, and unless we pick up any more injuries, that's where you'll stay. I've a responsibility to you, I know you've played more games than you should have. At times we've had no choice. But this time, we do."

Liam listened carefully and let the words wash over him. Once again, he knew Harry was right. To him, Harry was like a father. He trusted him completely, and he knew that he had his best interests at heart.

"Thanks Boss, for the talk I mean. And, for everything," said Liam.

"No worries, and, if you're anything like me when you can't play, stop off on the way home and get some flowers for Lisa. You might have a bit of grovelling you need to do."

Liam smiled, that might be the best bit of advice Harry had ever given him. Although flowers might not quite do it.

On Saturday, against Chorley, Clifton drew again. It was a game that was crying out for some inspiration from Liam, but Liam stayed seated on the bench. You could tell the crowd weren't happy, but Liam was fine. He had made his peace with the situation and was now concentrating on being fully ready for the last two league games and the cup final. A week later,

England drew 0-0 against Norway in Oslo. Jason was named man of the match while Chippy again remained in his tracksuit on the bench. It meant that, with just two qualifying games to go, England had to do the unthinkable. They had to travel to Rotterdam in June and beat the Flying Dutchmen in their own backyard, something that had not happened for more than three years. SS Milan had just been crowned Serie A league champions for the fourth year running and were in the final of the European Cup. Bakker, Van Den Berg and Hendrix had all been named in the FIFA world team of the year. England fans were already preparing themselves for more heartache.

Chapter Fifty-three

For Clifton, the league season practically crawled to a finish on the 8th of May. They drew their last two games to finish the season without a win in seven games. Liam was slowly returning to full fitness; he had played an hour in the penultimate game and had managed to last the full ninety minutes of the last game. The team received a great send-off from the Clifton fans, who could see the effort and application that the players had put into the season. Every one of them was on their last legs. They did receive some good news when their FA Cup Final opponents managed to score a last-gasp goal on the final day to clinch their first title in more than seventy years. Harwood Rovers had upset the big guns at Tottenford and Mansford. This was especially good news for Clifton Rangers. It now meant that whatever happened in the FA Cup Final, Clifton would be back in Europe next year. Taking their place in the Cup Winner's Cup. Harwood Rovers had only been back in the top division for four years, but they had received huge investment from their Chairman, Jim Walker. It was clubs like Harwood that really brought home Clifton's shortcomings to Harry. He wasn't looking for the millions that Jim Walker had splashed out. Just a decent amount of money to get a squad together that could compete. He knew that players like Chippy, Liam and Jason were going to outgrow Clifton very soon without the necessary investment. Even Whelan, O'Boyle and Panton wouldn't hang around for too long if matters were to carry on stagnating. Their final position had been thirteenth, three places lower than the previous year. He then looked at Harwood. Even though they were league champions, the rumour mill was still running overtime. Apparently, Walker had agreed to make the funds available for a big marquee signing in the summer. A signing that was intended to take the club to the next level. The rumours said that it was down to a straight choice between two young British prospects:
Dean Beadle and Liam Osborne.

Chapter Fifty-four

On a beautiful sunny afternoon, the sort of day that seemed to almost be reserved for the FA Cup Final, Harwood Rovers won their first FA Cup Final. It was a game too far for Clifton Rangers, who were second best throughout. Harwood Rovers had a huge squad, especially in comparison with Clifton, and their players had been rotated throughout the season. They looked fresh and sharp. Clifton, on the other hand, looked exactly what they were, exhausted and needing a break. Liam looked sharper than he had done for weeks, but Clifton just couldn't get the ball to him on enough occasions. The game finished 3-0 and that was probably just about right.

Clifton had finished the season with a whimper. Eight games without winning. Even with the disappointing end to the season, the press had still been full of praise for the job Harry was doing. He had somehow managed to get them to a second consecutive final, into Europe and had managed to get three of his players into the England squad. No-one spoke about Clifton without a *considering* or a *despite* or some other caveat. With what they had spent, and the size of their squad it was a miracle they had even stayed in the division. A season that had seen them start so well had petered out to mediocrity, but no-one was critical of the players or the staff. It seemed like the plucky Clifton Rangers were everyone's second favourite team.

After the game, Harry congratulated every one of his players and thanked them for their commitment over the season. He told them to go away, rest and recuperate. He spoke of the new challenge of European football. Long after the last player had left, Harry stood alone with his thoughts. To the players he had always remained positive and energetic, but in truth he was exhausted too. Without the proper backing, he wasn't sure that he could continue. His back-up plan had stalled and may never come to fruition. He felt like he was on the edge and all it would take was one more nudge to send him over.

Chapter Fifty-five

To Liam Osborne,

You have been nominated in the PFA young players category and are invited to attend the 20th PFA Awards, at the Grosvenor House in London.

The letter was brief but welcome. Liam and Lisa could do with a night out, and they both had fond memories of the last awards ceremony. This time, Liam had not kept it a secret as he was already keeping one secret from Lisa, and he thought he might explode if he tried to keep another.

Jason had also been nominated and so they all travelled into London together in Jason's car.

It was to be a great night, which started when Jason pulled up outside Liam and Lisa's home.

The sound of the horn made them both aware of Jason's arrival. Lisa was still putting in her earrings as she left the house. She was wearing a beautiful black dress and high heels. Her hair was down, and she had taken Liam's breath away when she came down the stairs. Despite Lisa's protests, Liam hired exactly the same tuxedo as the previous year. He didn't see the sense in buying one or looking to see what else was out there. Besides, he was sure that Dean Beadle was going to win. He had been the top scorer for the third year on the spin, and if you added in his four goals for England against San Marino, it seemed a certainty that he would pick up his third consecutive Young Player of the Year award. Jason beeped his horn again and Lisa and Liam hurried to the car. When they got in, the sight that greeted them was priceless. Jason had obviously watched last year's event. He had on the exact same outfit as Beadle had worn the previous year. Even down to the shades. His hair was also slicked back in the same style as Beadle, and he had a sneer on his face that was vintage Beadle. It set the tone for the night, by the time they had found a space and parked, Liam's sides ached from laughter. He was almost disappointed to see that he wasn't at Beadle's table. But even from across the room, he could see that Jason's outfit had attracted Beadle's attention. He looked about ready to explode, and if looks could kill, then Jason would not have even made it to his table. On his arm, Beadle had a different page three model from last year, he clearly had a type.

"We should enjoy this while we can, he's going to be a nightmare when he wins again," said Liam.

"I wouldn't be so sure," said Blackie.

"Oh come on, I've hardly been lifting up any trees recently. Don't forget his four goals against San Marino too…"

"No mate, think back. When did you cast your vote?"

"You're right Blackie, it must have been back in March. That's ages ago, way before the San Marino game."

"Exactly mate. You think he looks annoyed now. Imagine what he's going to look like if you win the award!"

At this they all looked across at Beadle, they were beginning to think that this could be an even better night than they had imagined.

Before long, the PFA chief, Gordon Webster, made his way onto the stage.

As with the previous year, the five players were introduced, and a short video montage showed some of their best moments from the season. Jason was the only defender nominated, so while the other four had some great goals and skills shown, Jason was shown making tackles and headers.

"Rock and roll mate, rock and roll," whispered Jason to Liam after a clip of another clearance. After each montage, the camera zoomed in on the nominee's face. When the camera crew moved in on Jason, he pulled his very best Beadle sneer. Lisa nearly spat out her drink with laughter.

Then came the announcement.

"And, this year's winner of the PFA Young Player of the Year is… Liam Osborne."

Liam's face was a picture. He did a comical double-take. Lisa and Jason both gave him a hug before he made his way up on stage to receive the award. It was all he could do to not laugh out loud as he was given the award by Gordon Webster. From up the front, he was treated to a double dose of Beadle sneer, it was comedy gold. Beadle had left before Liam got back to his seat.

By the time they got home, and waved goodbye to Jason, Lisa and Liam were tired but happy. The night had been just what they needed. During the season it had been like a rollercoaster, one thing after another dragging them along. Liam passed his award to Lisa.

"Hold this for a second," he said.

Lisa thought he was just getting the keys for the front door, but he pulled out an envelope that he passed to Lisa.

"What is it?" she asked.

"Open it and see."

Lisa fumbled with the envelope, eventually opening it to reveal another envelope, this time with the words Thomas Cook on the side and pictures of people on beaches and laying in the sun. She looked inside.

"A holiday, in Ibiza! Oh, Liam you shouldn't have. The Dutch game's soon, and you need to keep training."

"Howard Taylor rang after the cup final, he told me that I wasn't in the squad. Told me I'd not played enough football recently. That I'd looked short of match fitness. I didn't argue. Said that with my knee, he didn't want to risk me unless he had to," said Liam. "Look, anyway, I want this to be our time. I want to get away from football, spend some time with you. I've booked us into a lovely hotel in San Antonio right by the beach. It should be dead romantic, sitting on the beach in the day, eating out in the evening. A bit of peace and quiet, away from all the attention."

"I'm not going to lie, it sounds wonderful, but how did you afford it?"

"Another secret Harry clause. It was the game against San Marino. My first cap, another five grand bonus. I didn't say anything as I wanted it to be a surprise."

"£5,000, Liam that's great news. We'll easily have enough for us to finish decorating and kitting out the house."

Liam pretended he didn't hear the last comment.

Chapter Fifty-six

Liam first began to worry when he was sitting, waiting to board the plane. He felt old, everyone seemed to be younger than him. The only ones who seemed his age were in hen parties or stag parties. There were groups of nuns, lifeguards out of Baywatch, there was even a Wookie walking around. It was a night flight, and the smell of alcohol already filled the air. Liam tried to avoid Lisa's gaze. The truth was he had never booked a holiday before so when he went in the travel agents, he just told the pimply youth behind the counter that he wanted to go to Spain and be near a beach. He had heard the other players talking about their trips in the off-season, and they always seemed to go to Spain. He didn't quite realise how big the Spanish coast was, or how diverse the holiday destinations were. When he was sitting waiting, he noticed some of the groups of stags, or was it a herd, looking in his direction. He slipped his sunglasses out of his pocket and pulled his cap down further, hoping to remain anonymous.

Eventually, they boarded and took their seats.

"Bit of a squeeze isn't it?" said Lisa.

She had only travelled on a plane with her dad before. They never travelled cattle class.

A plane full of drunk, loud passengers wasn't a pleasant experience. The queue for the bathroom never seemed to go down. Liam and Lisa's seats were four rows from the bathroom, and so their chairs were constantly being knocked and jolted. Stag and hen parties were scattered about the plane, but that didn't stop them talking, often over the top of where Liam and Lisa were trying to sleep. Liam squirmed in his seat. Maybe their hotel would be in a different place far away from the party-seekers on the plane.

When they landed, and after they collected their bags, they followed the signs to the coach that would transfer them to their hotel. It was about two in the morning by that time, and both Liam and Lisa just wanted to get to the hotel as quickly as possible. The holiday rep at the door of the coach crossed off their names, and they boarded. The clientele was different from most of the people on the plane.

It was worse.

Liam was watching them get on the coach and it was clear that they were looking for a different kind of holiday to him. San Antonio had sounded like such an exclusive place. Then came his worst nightmare. A group of boisterous lads boarded the coach and started making their way down the central aisle. There was about eight or nine of them, they were clearly already drunk, and they were all wearing Netfield County shirts. Lisa spotted them too, she squeezed Liam's hand. Liam tried to slide down in his seat.

"I don't think they recognised you," said Lisa after they passed them and made their way to the back of the coach.

"We hate Clifton and we hate Clifton we hate Clifton and we hate Clifton. we are the Clifton haters!"

"Then again maybe not," said Lisa.

The Netfield fans did not let up for one second, even targeting some of their songs specifically at Liam, songs that weren't very complimentary. Lisa and Liam took to looking out the window. Every now and then, the coach would pull up outside a hotel and a few holiday makers would disembark. Lisa and Liam would check out the hotel. The comments ranged from "That one looks nice," or "Don't fancy that one," to "What a dump." No prizes for guessing which one was theirs. As a bonus, it was also the Netfield fans' hotel too. The rep took them into their hotel and checked them in.

"The manager's a grumpy git who doesn't speak much English, but your hotel rep's name is Garry. Any problems, go straight to him, he can sort it out for you."

Lisa was trying to stay positive; she knew that Liam had wanted this to be a special time for the two of them.

"Well, at least the room's okay," she remarked as they opened the door.

It was a nice room, if a little basic. They also had a balcony that overlooked the pool. They both dumped their bags and went out to look. The temperature was still in the eighties, despite it being the middle of the night, practically the morning. From the balcony they could see out over the pool and down over the town to the sea. The water shimmered under the moonlight.

"Oh Liam, this *is* so romantic."

Liam put his hand out to take Lisa's hand.

"Waaaheeey!!"

The cry came from below them. Next thing they knew, the calm water of their pool was broken by the bodies of eight burly Northerners diving into the water.

"Shall we go to bed?" asked Liam.

"Yes, I think maybe we should," came the reply.

They felt as if their heads had only just touched the pillows when a banging on the door rudely awoke them. Liam stumbled out of bed, knocking over and breaking the lamp on the table next to him. He grabbed a towel to put round him, and found his way to the door, barely awake. He put on the chain and partly opened the door, looking around the corner. There was an overly happy looking rep with too much gel in his hair standing there. He looked like an excitable puppy.

"Hi guys," he said craning his neck trying to look past Liam into the room. "Are you coming to the excursion meeting?"

"Excursion meeting, what do you mean? What time is it?"

The rep ignored both questions.

"Down in the restaurant area, guys."

"What do you mean excursions?" Liam tried again.

"Club 18-30? We have the Sangria pool party this afternoon guys, the pub crawl tonight, the…"

"Club 18-30? I didn't… you mean this is… Look, we aren't interested, can you give us some peace? We've only just got here; I'm going back to bed."

Liam didn't wait for an answer and closed the door on the rep, who looked most put out.

He then stumbled back to the bed, just about making out the time on the clock as he went. 7.00am. He had been in bed for about three hours.

As he lay back down, Lisa flopped an arm onto his back, and without opening her eyes, she mumbled, "Garry Guys?"

"Yep!"

"Club 18-30, good job, Mr Osborne."

Then they both fell back to sleep.

162

They were woken again at about nine. The pool had obviously opened, and they could hear the mad rush for loungers from their room.

"I guess it's time to get up," said Lisa.

Liam stuck a pillow over his head, but to no avail.

"I guess so," he said.

After they had showered and dressed, they decided to wander down to the beach and explore.

As they made their way through reception, they broke into a jog, trying to avoid the Netfield fans, who they could hear down by the pool.

To get to the beach they had to walk through San Antonio town, which could be summed up in five words: alcohol, alcohol, food, rubbish and alcohol. The cleaners looked to be still cleaning up from the night before. Meanwhile, there seemed to be an awful lot of people already starting their night. At 10:12 in the morning.

Liam and Lisa started to play a game they called drunk bingo. Every time one of them spotted a drunk person, they got a point. Extremely drunk was worth two, but only if the other person agreed. By the time they reached the beach, Liam was winning thirty-four points to thirty-one.

The beach itself wasn't that busy, so they grabbed a bit of breakfast on the waterfront then hired out a couple of deckchairs and a parasol. Liam was glad he had his sunglasses on, as the women on the beach were wearing next to nothing and he didn't know where to look. He was drifting in and out of sleep when he noticed that quite a lot of the girls seemed to be looking at him. It became quite comical. The girls were walking up and down the beach as if they were models on a catwalk, every now and then glancing in Liam's direction. It seemed most of the sunbathers were English, and clearly a lot of them were football fans. Feeling guilty, Liam looked across at Lisa. She was oblivious to the whole thing, busy sun worshipping. Liam decided to close his eyes again, and it wasn't long before he drifted off to sleep. Later, when he woke up, he noticed that their bit of beach seemed to be busier than anywhere else. It was like they were a magnet pulling everything towards them. All the loungers seemed to be pointed in their direction. He no longer needed to look around at

163

the scantily clad women, it seemed that if the mountain wouldn't go to Muhammad…

It was at about this point that Liam also started to notice that some of the beefcakes along the beach were looking in his direction, too. Liam wasn't sure if they wanted to fight him or date him. He decided he didn't want to wait around to find out.

"Lisa, Lisa, wake up. I think it's time we made a move." Liam reached across and shook Lisa by the arm.

When Lisa first woke up, Liam could see she was a bit irritated at being woken, but when she looked around her, she soon decided that she didn't want to be there either.

"It's like being a goldfish in a bowl, except all the eyes are on the more expensive fish next to you," she said.

"It's getting a bit overcast, anyway," said Liam.

And he was right, the clouds had really started to thicken. They had to run the last part of the walk to the hotel to avoid being completely drenched. They were only partly successful.

"Well, you got a bit of a run in I guess," said Lisa. "Not quite along the beach as you imagined though."

Liam went to reply, but seeing Lisa standing their soaked to the skin, wet hair plastered to her forehead, he couldn't find the words. Instead, he just broke into a fit of laughter. Liam's laughter set Lisa off too and before long they both had tears rolling down their already wet faces.

"So, what's next on your master plan Mr Osborne? We could get the full English experience. Maybe a night in the cells? Or maybe an excursion 'guys'?"

"Very funny. Well, this rain seems set for the duration maybe we could get some snacks from the supermarket we walked past."

"When you say *we*, I'm sure you meant to say *I*. I know how gallant you are, Mr Osborne, you wouldn't send a dog out in this weather, let alone the love of your life."

"As I was saying. *I* could go back to the supermarket we passed and get *us* some snacks. I still feel knackered from the flight, maybe a romantic night in the room wouldn't be such a bad thing."

"Romantic? What's got into you Mr Osborne? You don't normally have a romantic bone in your body."

"Must be the weather," said Liam setting off to the supermarket.

When he returned with the snacks, he could see Lisa talking to rep Garry at the entrance to the hotel.

"What did Garry 'guys' want?" asked Liam.

"I couldn't get rid of him. He did say there was a lovely little bar that did food out on the edge of the water though 'guys'. Apparently, all the locals go there and watch the sunset. It's a thing in Ibiza, they watch the sunset every night. I thought maybe we could go there tomorrow if the rain's gone."

"Sounds perfect."

As they made their way through the lobby, the Spanish man at reception shouted something aggressively at them in Spanish.

"Sorry, we do not understand Spanish," said Liam, very loudly and deliberately. "E N G L I S H?"

He clearly understood about as much English as they did Spanish. But It didn't discourage the manager, who continued gesturing and shouting at them in very fast Spanish.

In the end, they waved at him, smiled and continued on their way.

"What's his problem?" asked Lisa.

"You don't reckon it's the lamp, do you?"

"Oh God, I bet it is. We better stay out of his way."

"Great, so now it's the Netfield massive, Garry 'guys' the rep and the hotel manager we want to avoid. Maybe we should just get a disguise. You'd look good with a beard," said Liam.

Lisa's reply came in the form of a dig to the ribs.

In the end, they had a great night. Liam had bought some cards in the supermarket, so they spent the night playing cards and eating Spanish snacks and laughing hysterically at English sweets with Spanish names. The next day they were woken at seven by Garry the rep, inviting them down for the excursion meeting. The greeting he receive from Liam was enough to guarantee that it wouldn't be happening again, much to Lisa's amusement.

"Someone's not a morning person," she said. "How's the weather?"

"Great," said Liam. "If you're a duck."

When they finally got up, they ate the rest of the snacks and sat on the balcony watching the world go by.

"This is so-" started Liam.

"Romantic? Who are you? What have you done with my Liam? The only thing he ever got misty eyed over was Match of the Day."

Eventually, the clouds began to part.

"At least we'll be able to go down to that bar Garry 'guys' recommended and watch the sunset," said Liam.

"Yeah, sounds dead romantic eh? If we can sneak past everyone. Did you buy a disguise at the supermarket?"

After they had showered and changed, they made their way down to the lobby area. They could see the Netfield posse drinking at the hotel bar so were able to sneak past them without too much trouble.

"He's behind reception," whispered Liam.

"There's no other way out, we are going to have to just go for it," said Lisa.

"Okay, heads down and just keep walking."

The manager spotted them again, and like before he was off in a continuous flow of unintelligible Spanish. All the while gesticulating wildly with his arms. At one point, Liam was sure he heard his name, but he didn't slow down long enough to know for sure.

It was about a ten-minute walk to the bar and Garry's directions had been spot on. The bar was packed. It was a beautiful little white building practically on the rocks next to the sea. The locals were scattered along the rocks, they had brought their own food and drink and were waiting for the sunset.

"Can we have a table with a view of the sunset please," asked Liam.

The waiter showed them to a table with a great view across the bay. Lisa ordered a glass of red wine, and Liam had a bottle of sparkling water. They ordered some tapas and sat watching the sun slowly set across the bay. It was a stunning sight; the whole sky was a beautiful blend of purples and reds.

"Okay Osborne, you've got me this time. If it was romance you were after, then you've succeeded. I don't think I'm ever going to forget this moment."

Liam reached across and took Lisa by the hand, looking into her eyes.

"Liam Osborne!? No way! What are you doing here?" came the shout from across the restaurant. A shaven-headed, heavily tattooed man came charging across the bar, spilling his pint of lager as he went.

"Err, hi, I'm just having a rom.., I mean a meal with my girlfriend. I was just," stammered Liam with his normal eloquence.

"No, no, I *literally* mean what are you doing *here*? You're supposed to be in Holland."

"What?!" said both Liam and Lisa at the same time.

The man nipped back to his own table and returned with a copy of The Globe.

"Look," he said. "Right there, three forwards have dropped out of the squad. It says you've been called up. Look, they've even put you in their expected starting eleven!"

He was right, clear as day, there was Liam's name. Dean Beadle was the only recognised forward left in the squad. If Taylor was going to stick to a four-four-two formation, and he always did, then the chances are that it would Liam and Beadle up front. The game was on Saturday and it was already Wednesday evening.

"Oh my God, Lisa, what are we going to do?"

"Well first of all you need to pay the bill, then we need to get you on a flight back to England!"

"Have you finished with this?" asked Liam, pointing to the newspaper.

"Yeah of course, take it. Good luck, we can't have a World Cup without the three lions in it!"

Garry the rep turned out to be quite the hero. He was a Clifton fan, and he went above and beyond to make sure that Liam got home as quickly as possible. It turned out that the angry hotel manager wasn't angry at all. He had been trying to let Liam know that he there had been a whole bunch of phone calls from the UK for him.

It had all been arranged. Liam would be landing at Luton at two in the morning. He was then booked on a flight to Rotterdam at 6.30 that morning. Apparently, Liam's mum had been round to their house and got Liam's boots and shinpads and given them to Jason, who had already taken them out to Holland.

When they got to Luton, Lisa stayed with Liam until the next flight. The airport was deserted.

"I'm so sorry Lisa, this wasn't how I had it planned. I so wanted this week to be special."

"Don't be daft, I loved every second. I'm so excited for you, Liam. Your full debut. That's all you need to think about now. Making sure you're ready for the game," said Lisa. "Have you got everything?"

"I think so."

"How about your passport? You're screwed if you haven't got that."

"Yes, it's in the pocket on my backpack."

"Okay, just let me check for you," said Lisa, grabbing Liam's bag and unzipping the pocket.

"NO! Stop, don't open..." began Liam, but it was too late.

"W... what's this?" said Lisa. She was holding a small red box with Ernest Jones written on top.

She looked up from it to Liam, there was a tear in her eye as the reality dawned on her.

"Liam, is th... is this?"

Liam slid down from his chair, so he was on the floor kneeling in front of her.

"Liam, get up, your knee."

"The knee's fine Lisa. Let me at least do this properly. I've spent two days trying to find the perfect moment. The most *romantic* moment."

Lisa blushed.

Liam carried on, "I never thought that the waiting area in a deserted Luton airport would be where I was doing this. But... Lisa Salow, will you do me the honour of becoming Mrs Osborne?"

Liam took the box from Lisa's shaking hand and flipped it open to reveal a platinum ring with a large sparkling diamond protruding from it.

"Liam, this must have cost you a fortune."

"About the same price as a decorated and fully kitted out maisonette, apparently. Now will you give me an answer, so I can get up off this filthy floor?"

"Yes... yes, yes, YES!" said Lisa flinging her arms around Liam. "I can't think of anything I want more."

Chapter Fifty-seven

The newly engaged Liam Osborne was met at the Hague airport, Rotterdam, by a representative of the FA who whisked him away to the team's hotel.

"There is a training session this morning at eleven. Mr Taylor instructed me to tell you that the training kit is in your room and the coach is leaving at 10.45," said the man from the FA. "Mr Taylor has delayed the session so that you can be there."

Liam checked his watch. 10.24. It was turning into an awfully long, stressful day.

Jason was already changed for training when Liam got to his room.

"Hiya Blackie, you got my boots?" asked Liam.

"Yeah mate, on the chair over there, with your kit."

Liam quickly got changed, he only had a few minutes before they needed to be down in the lobby ready for the coach. Blackie seemed noticeably quiet. Normally, Liam couldn't shut him up, but he seemed a little distracted. Liam grabbed his boots.

"You okay Blackie?" said Liam.

"Yeah, I'm okay. I mean there is something I need to talk to you about mate. But I'm good."

"Okay, we can chat on the coach. We better rush now though or we'll be late. I've got some pretty big news of my own!"

Most of the players were in the lobby when Liam and Blackie got there. They both saw Chippy and started to make their way over to him.

"Here he is. Glad you could finally make it," Dean Beadle wasted no time. "You saying your goodbyes?"

"Shut up, Dean," Jason stepped forward, putting himself between Liam and Beadle.

"What? You not told him yet?" said Beadle.

"It's just a rumour," said Jason.

"Not what my agent says. He reckons it's a done deal. Who knows, we might be teammates at Harwood next year. What a turn up for the books that would be!"

"Harwood Rovers? Since when?" asked Liam.

"That's what I was going to talk to you about, mate. Got a phone call from the FA's English press office this morning, said that Harwood had made a bid for me. Asking if I wanted to comment."

"What did your agent really say then?" said Liam to Beadle.

"He told me that Jimmy Walker was looking to sign a defender and a forward. He said that Blackie is all but done. Then it's me or you as the forward, and we all know that you're never leaving Clifton. Which means I'm about to become the best-paid player in British football."

"Right lads, coach is here; everyone on."

The sound of Howard Taylor meant that the conversation finished, and all the players made their way out onto the coach. Liam and Jason sat next to each other near the front.

"What will you do?" asked Liam.

"I don't know, mate. I'm not like you. You've supported Clifton your whole life. Don't get me wrong, I love playing for Clifton, we have a great bunch of lads. But I look at other clubs and how they treat their players and it's not right. We never stay overnight before a game; we get paid way less than everyone else, we don't even have a reserve team. I would be too embarrassed to say how much we get paid in front of this lot. I mean, Jesus Liam, we're playing for England and I bet they all earn more in a week than I do in a month. Harwood did the double last year and they're in the European Cup next year."

"We're in the Cup Winners Cup," said Liam.

"Yeah mate, without winning a cup! And you know what that's going to be like. We'll probably have to go by coach and sleep in a tent. I'm not saying that I would definitely go if they do come in for me. But I'm not saying I wouldn't."

Liam never even mentioned his own news.

Training was just a light session. It had been a long, hard season and Taylor was of the mind that if the players weren't fit now, then they would never be. Most of the session was just working on team shape. This did mean that the starting eleven was clear. Jason would start at centre half, while Liam would partner Beadle up front. It meant that, once again, Chippy would be on the bench.

As soon as they got back to the hotel, Liam rang Lisa.

"Hello, Lisa? Have you heard anything about Blackie?"

"I have, but it's not good Liam. Apparently, Dad wants to sell him. Stuart says that Harry and him had a blazing row, he could hear it right down the corridor. Stuart says that Dad's secretary heard Harry tell my dad that if Jason goes, he goes too," Lisa paused to let Liam take it all in. It sounded like gossip in a playground. "Liam, my Dad's the most stubborn person I know. There's no way he'll back down."

"Not Harry, it's bad enough if Blackie goes, but if Harry leaves. Lisa, I don't know what I'd do."

"Hmm, I wasn't going to say anything. From my point of view, obviously, it's easier if we stay in Clifton. We have the new house. Your mum and my dad are nearby. And we both love and support the team. But, that said, things change quickly in football, and I'll support you in whatever you decide."

"What is it? What you not telling me?"

"Well, Stuart said he'd also heard another rumour. He's been told that as well as bidding for Blackie, Harwood Rovers also made an official enquiry about your availability. The way he spoke, it sounds like you're their first choice, not Dean Beadle."

"Oh Lisa, my head's spinning. I wish you were here."

"Glad you said that because when I heard all this, I booked myself on a flight to Rotterdam. I should be there tomorrow afternoon. I just wanted to be near you, and I couldn't miss your full debut. In one of England's most important games."

"Oh God! I'd almost forgotten the game." said Liam.

Chapter Fifty-eight

The atmosphere on the way to the game was electric. The coach was due to get to the ground at 1.00pm, ready for a 3.00pm kick off. In the end, it didn't get there until 1.45pm because of a sea of orange that it had to negotiate. There were fans everywhere, the national team had really captured the nation's imagination and they had come out in force to support them, with and without a ticket.

It was going to be a tough ask of England. They had to win to stand any chance of qualification, but no-one was really giving them a chance. The only real positive was the fact that, with a few players dropping out, it was a young and hungry English team that took the field in the Feyenoord Stadium in front of 51,000 partisan fans. Other than a small corner of the stadium, the terraces were awash with orange.

As he waited to take kick off, Liam tried to take it all in. Across from him were the Milan three, Van Den Berg, Bakker and Hendrix. Liam knew of their ability but was surprised to see how physically imposing they were. All three of them of them were well over six feet tall, and an aura of confidence radiated from them. Liam looked down at his shirt, the famous three lions emblazoned across his chest. He glanced up to the main stand where he knew Lisa would be sitting. Suddenly, it was like he was back on the marshes, playing for any team that would have him. That's all it was, just another game. Another step on the path. A calmness surrounded him. He knew, without a moment's doubt, that today was his day. That this was the place he was meant to be. Then the whistle blew, and they were off. The first fifteen minutes were like a game of chess, both teams feeling each other out, vying for position. Van Den Berg was trying everything he knew to get some space, but Jason was stuck to his side. Physically, they were a good match, both sitting at about six foot three and both possessing a good turn of pace. It was clear that the Dutch forward was not used to playing against an equal and was already getting frustrated. In attack, Liam and Beadle were looking dangerous, they had linked up well on a few occasions. It was only the positional play of Frank Bakker that had so far prevented England from creating any clear openings. He always seemed to sense the danger and be there before an attack could become too dangerous. The problems for England were all coming from the centre of the pitch and from one man, Ruud Hendrix. England were outnumbered in midfield, three to two. Hendrix was having a field day with the space he was finding. One minute he would be getting the ball off his own defenders, the next he would be picking the ball up in attack beyond the English midfield. Gradually, the game was being clawed away from England. The Dutch were starting to dominate possession. Hendrix was dictating everything; he was enjoying himself. After half of an hour, it looked like it was going to be a long day for England. Chances were starting to be created and they were all at England's end. In the thirty-fourth minute, Hendrix managed to break free from the English midfield and was now running at the English back four. As he approached the edge of the box, Jason had no choice but to leave Van Den Berg and close down the onrushing Hendrix, trying to prevent him from getting a shot away. Hendrix had been waiting for this. The moment Jason left Van Den Berg's side, Hendrix reversed the ball into the big Dutch forward's path. The finish was exemplary. 1-0 to the Dutch in a game that England had to win.

The rest of the half was the Ruud Hendrix show. With space to play in, it became like a keep-ball exercise. The statistics showed that Hendrix finished the first half with nearly a hundred touches, while Beadle and Liam had less than twenty between them.

Changes had to be made at half time if England were going to get back into the game. It was surely time for Taylor to step away from his favoured four-four-two formation.

"Lads, we are getting murdered in the middle of the park. I'm going to freshen it up a bit. Chippy, get yourself outside and get warmed up. You're going on."

It was a straight swap, like for like. Liam and Jason exchanged looks, they knew that unless something was done about Hendrix then nothing much was going to change.

"Now get back out there, get the ball to Liam and Dean, they've got goals in them," said Taylor.

As Liam and Jason made their way back out onto the pitch, they shared their concerns.

"Liam, mate, they're outnumbering us in the middle. Hendrix is strolling around like he owns the place."

"I know but what we supposed to do. I-"

"Right, forget what he says, I've waited too long for this moment to let it slip away," it was Chippy, intercepting them both as they got to pitch side. "Liam, get yourself back in the middle with me. Start getting around Hendrix, let's upset him a bit."

"But Chippy, Howard said…"

"I know what he said, Liam, but he's wrong. Unless we do something about it, we're going out without even a whimper. You know I'm right. Let's argue about this later," said Chippy.

Liam looked at Jason, who nodded, showing that he agreed.

"Okay, sod it. It's not like it's my full debut or anything. I'm with you Chippy, but you'd better be right."

Immediately, Liam dropping back had two effects. First, Hendrix was upset. He had been having things his own way and, suddenly, he had Chippy and Liam snapping away at him. England were beginning to get more of the ball. The minute they got it, they were off, breaking into attack. The second thing was that Howard Taylor was apoplectic on the touchline, screaming at Liam to get back up front. He clearly saw it as a disobeying his instructions. After ten minutes he sent out the substitutes to warm up. A clear message to Liam.

Liam got the message, but he had gone too far to back down now. Besides, he could see that it was working. Hendrix was getting more and more frustrated and England were beginning to look like the better side. Liam had managed to burst forward and support Beadle on several occasions and the England fans sensed that if England could get a goal, then they would go on and win the match. On the sideline, the substitutes were called back in and the substitution board was being set up.

The Dutch were still trying to play through Hendrix, who had started to drop deeper, playing just in front of his defence. On sixty-four minutes the Dutch right winger played a pass into the feet of Hendrix, but Chippy was ready. He slid across the pitch, just getting a toe to the ball, sending it spinning into the space between the Dutch defence and midfield. Liam was onto it in a flash. Beadle spun in behind for the ball over the top, Liam spotted him and played an early pass for him to run onto. Beadle was onto it in a second but was forced wide. The Dutch defender made the tackle, but Beadle was able to ride it and just about keep control of the ball. He was now on the left side of the area between the penalty spot and the touchline. A second Dutch defender had managed to close him down and prevent any shot coming in.

"Dean cut it back!" screamed Liam as he arrived at the penalty spot.

Without looking, Beadle passed the ball in the direction of Liam's voice. It was perfect, straight into Liam's path. But Bakker had read it and was already sliding in to block the shot.

"Chippy's!" came the call from behind Liam.

Liam faked the shot and let the ball run through his legs to the arriving Clifton midfielder. All Chippy had to do was make a clean connection, the whole left-hand side of the goal was unprotected as everyone had been drawn towards Liam. Chippy made no mistake. 1-1, game on. Chippy did not stop running, he grabbed the ball from the back of the net and ran back to the halfway line, gesturing with his arms for the rest of his team to do the same. The job wasn't finished yet.

On the side-line, the substitutes were told to sit back down again.

It was another ten minutes before the next chance was created. The Dutch had changed tactics and were getting more and more people behind the ball. Trying to play out the last twenty minutes. A neat one-two had seen Beadle get a sight of goal, but a tug on his shirt had prevented him from getting his shot away. It did, however, mean a free kick in a dangerous position.

"I've got it," said Liam, jogging over.

"No, I won it, I'll take it," said Beadle grabbing and holding onto the ball.

Liam had already had one defiant moment and wasn't sure if he had another one in him, so he relented. Beadle placed the ball carefully, paced out his run up, and waited for the whistle. As the whistle blew, he began his run up, it was a clean strike and arced over the wall, but it was too central. The Dutch keeper was able to deal with it comfortably.

It was beginning to look like this was going to be the last chance of the game. As Liam had found throughout his career with Clifton, it was exceedingly difficult to play against a team that wasn't interested in trying to score. When the players were also as good as the Dutch were, it was almost impossible. They could not seem to find any space.

All the while the clock was ticking away.

England's main threat was now set pieces. They were winning a lot of free kicks and corners as the Dutch players threw themselves into tackles. The problem was that the Dutch were a huge side and were able to deal comfortably with any crosses that came into the box. The other problem was Dean Beadle. He had taken to shooting from every free kick that England were awarded. He must have had four efforts in the final twenty minutes, at least three of which were beyond optimistic.

The huge clock at the Feyenoord stadium showed 4.45, meaning that the ninety minutes were up. All that was left was any stoppage time the referee decided to add. It was another corner, again the Dutch dealt with the cross comfortably, this time with a clearing header from Bakker. Chippy, though, had been waiting for it. He had seen how dominant the Dutch had been aerially. He was interested in the second ball, he moved up from his position on the halfway line and was now on the edge of the box as the ball dropped. Chippy shut out everything around him, concentrating only on his connection with the ball.

He struck it perfectly.

Out of nowhere, a desperate, sliding Hendrix managed to get his body in the way of the shot. The English players went mad, surrounding the referee. They were convinced that Hendrix had used his arm. But the referee was on the wrong side of the challenge, there was no way he could have seen it. Once again, England were to be denied by a 'Hand of God'. The referee may have been on the wrong side of the ball, but the Russian linesman was not. Eventually, the English players managed to get the referee's attention to the waving flag of his linesman. After a brief consultation, the decision was made. A free kick on the edge of the box. Now it was the Dutch players' turn to surround the referee. Some were disputing the decision, while others were pointing to imaginary watches, clearly feeling that the time was up. Tellingly, Hendrix was not disputing the award of the free kick. As the referee had given the free kick, he was now able to stretch out and flex his sore wrist.

Immediately, Beadle was there, ready to take the free kick. But this time he didn't have the ball. Jason did.

"I'm telling you now, mate, you'll have to prise this ball out of my dead hands. Now sod off out the way. Liam's got this one."

Whether it was Jason's tone, the look on his face or the fact that he towered over Beadle that did the trick, it was hard to say.

Beadle didn't argue.

Liam called over Chippy.

"You know what to do," he said.

Chippy nodded.

The Dutch keeper lined up the wall and then returned to his side of the goal. Then three things happened almost simultaneously. Chippy picked up the ball and took a step to his left, before putting the ball back down. The Dutch keeper sprinted back across his goal to realign the wall. Liam looked at the referee, asking the question.

The slight nod from the referee's head was all that Liam needed. No sooner had the ball left his right boot than Liam was off, running. His hours of practice in the ball court meant he knew when he had made a clean connection. The Dutch keeper changed direction and launched himself at the ball, but he knew that he wasn't going to make it. In truth, he never got close. The ball hitting the back of the net was followed by Liam arriving at the small corner of the stadium where a few hundred English fans were going berserk. The whole English team, even Dean Beadle, soon joined him. It was a shared moment of ecstasy that was echoed in living rooms and pubs throughout England. It was in stark contrast to the 50,000-plus Dutch fans who were now silent. The sea of orange had hit a dam.

As Liam finally made his way back to the halfway line, ready for the game to restart, he waved up to the main stand where he knew Lisa was. He had not expected to see her, but he wanted her to know he was thinking of her at this special moment in his life. But he did. She was standing amongst thousands of seated fans, with a smile that he would have spotted in an ocean of smiles. It was a moment he would never forget.

The game kicked off and before three passes could be completed the final whistle went. England had all-but guaranteed their place in the World Cup Finals in America, in almost exactly a year's time.

In a true compliment, Ruud Hendrix made a beeline to Liam at the final whistle.

"You are special player, I'm sure we meet again. Would like swap shirts?" he asked in broken English.

"It would be an honour, thank you," said Liam.

Chapter Fifty-nine

The away changing room in the Feyenoord Stadium was alive with excitement. There was champagne, cheering and singing. Chippy even managed to get Jason to do a verse and chorus of "Everything I Do." Liam tried to avoid Howard Taylor as much as possible, still aware that he had gone against instructions. He was almost relieved when he later saw an interview where Taylor took credit for the change of tactics. Liam was desperate to share the moment with Lisa, seeing her in the stand was an image that had stayed with him. He secretly checked his phone but had no signal.

Once they had changed, Liam and Jason made their way out of the changing rooms and set off for the player's lounge. As he walked, Liam could feel his phone vibrating over and over. When he checked it, he had eighty-seven missed calls. He guessed it would be people congratulating him for the goal. Before he made it to the players' lounge, he was met by a Dutch official in a suit, holding a piece of paper.

"Liam Osborne?" asked the Dutch official.

Liam nodded.

The Dutch official glanced at the paper.

"A Miss Salow is waiting for you in the reception area, she asked if you could meet her there."

"Thank you," Liam turned to Jason. "Blackie, I'm just off to meet Lisa, I'll bring her up to the players' lounge. See you in a minute."

Jason just nodded; he too was checking his phone.

The minute they saw each other they both ran across the hallway to embrace. Lisa had tears in her eyes, and she held him close. When they finally let go of each other, Liam could see that although Lisa was clearly overjoyed at what had happened, there was something else. Something that she needed to tell him.

"Look Liam, I had to talk to you before you got upstairs."

Lisa was interrupted by the sound of a door bursting open behind them. Two men carrying cameras hurried in. A few members of stadium security came running over trying to herd them back out.

"Liam, Liam can I get a quote," shouted one of the intruders. He was trying to take a picture while battling against the security team who were trying to repel him.

"I'm just so happy that we've qualified," called out Liam, confused by what was happening.

"Not on the game," said the other intruder. "About Harry Welch."

Before Liam could answer the two reporters were removed by the security team.

Liam looked back at Lisa, but her face already gave him the answer.

They had accepted the bid for Jason.

Harry Welch had resigned.

His best friend, Jason had been the one player who had been there for him from the start. A friend when he most needed one. Then there was Harry, his mentor, the man he thought of like a father. The man who had believed in him and taken him on this unbelievable journey. He could feel himself choking up. Lisa took him by the hand.

At the very moment of his greatest achievement, at the peak of his success, it was all suddenly clear.

It might be time to leave his Clifton Rangers.

Printed in Great Britain
by Amazon

78690128R00108